W9-CHT-719

LIFE OF ZARF

THE TROLL WHO CRIED WOLF

LIFE OF ZARF

THE TROLL WHO CRIED WOLF

ROB
HARRELL

DIAL BOOKS *for* YOUNG READERS
an imprint of Penguin Group (USA) LLC

DIAL BOOKS FOR YOUNG READERS
Published by the Penguin Group • Penguin Group (USA) LLC
375 Hudson Street • New York, New York 10014

USA | Canada | UK | Ireland | Australia | New Zealand | India | South Africa | China
penguin.com

A PENGUIN RANDOM HOUSE COMPANY

Library of Congress Cataloging-in-Publication Data
Harrell, Rob, author, illustrator.
The troll who cried wolf / by Rob Harrell.
pages cm. — (Life of Zarf ; 2)
Summary: Fractured fairy tales meet modern day middle school when Zarf's unpopular troll social status becomes the least of his problems as a gang of wolves seeking revenge for the constant disgrace they have suffered over the years kidnaps Kevin, one of Zarf's best friends.
ISBN 978-0-8037-4104-1 (hardback)
[1. Trolls—Fiction. 2. Wolves—Fiction. 3. Middle schools—Fiction. 4. Schools—Fiction.
5. Characters in literature—Fiction. 6. Humorous stories.] I. Title.
PZ7.H2348To 2015   [Fic]—dc23   2015008881

1 3 5 7 9 10 8 6 4 2
Designed by Jason Henry • Text set in Italian Old Style MT Std

For Bur

· 1 ·

LET THE
FESTIVITIES BEGIN

Sunscreen and fur do not mix well. It makes you look all clumpy and weird. It also makes you sticky, so you end up attracting dirt and trash and anything else you happen to wander by. I've been known to come home looking like a used lint roller.

But try telling that to my mom. The sun was shining bright as my family made our way to Littlepig

Manor, so she kept creeping up and spraying me in little sneak attacks.

My grandpa—Gramps, as he's known around the house—was humming his I'm-in-a-great-mood tune. Huff n Puff Day was one of his favorite days of the year.

"I plan on eatin' 'til I explode, lad! So best bring a shovel and some paper towels to clean up what's left o' me . . ."

But, maybe I should back up.

My full name is Zarf Belford. I live in the village of Cotswin, within the kingdom of Notswin. I'm a troll, currently slogging my way through the fun-house nightmare that is middle school. Unfortunately, trolls are about as welcome at Cotswin Middle School as mungworms in a bowl of fettuccini.

I'm surviving, though. Largely because of my best friends, Kevin and Chester.

I could tell you more—like about what a jerky little snot-basket my classmate Prince Roquefort is, but I think you'll see for yourself. I could give you the "Rules to Live By in the Kingdom of Notswin"—things like "Never pet a bubbling Fester Turtle"—but let's try to be at least a little organic here. Things will come up. You'll catch on. I promise.

So, once a year, Kevin's parents hold the Annual Huff n Puff Day Festival at their huge home, Littlepig Manor. It's a celebration of the Littlepigs' triumph over a certain huffing and puffing wolf some years ago, and it is—simply put—the greatest thing since ever and ever.

Anyway, the entire village of Cotswin shows up, as well as a good chunk of the rest of the kingdom. The Littlepigs have done incredibly well in the construction business (since giving up sticks and hay as building materials), and they go all out. There are games and music and stage shows. There's a Blow Down the House game, where you put on wolf ears and try to blow down a house made of twigs. They have ponies and carnival rides and a huge Ferris wheel and enough free food to send the whole crowd home holding their stomachs. There are mutton bowls, porridge cones, cotton candy, and deep-fried Grundle Bars.

GRUNDLE-ICIOUS!!

Which explains why my dad and Gramps decided to wear their elastic-waisted "Eatin' Pants." Their goal each year was to see how much free grub they could cram into their mutton holes, and they swore this year would be their finest moment. My gramps was rattling on about how he was going to win the Wolf Gut Pie–Eating Contest, though my mother was trying to talk him out of it. (I should tell you that there are no actual wolf guts in Wolf Gut Pie. It's just strawberry-rhubarb pie, renamed for this one day a year.)

NO WOLVES WERE HARMED IN THE MAKING OF THIS PIE.

UNFORTUNATELY.

If eating pies made to look like wolf guts seems harsh, you should know that wolves are just the worst. Seriously, they're vicious, sneaky, angry eating machines. They've been a problem since time began. Maybe before. Wolf attacks. People getting eaten. Flea infestations. But in recent years they've been shunned from decent society and tend to run around the wilderness in motorcycle gangs—living the criminal life.

Then there was the worst of all wolves, the infamous Big Bad Wolf. He's the boogeyman parents tell their kids about to get them in bed at night.

At the very least, I'm sure you've heard of him—years ago he blew down the Littlepigs' homes until they finally held him off with a house made of brick.

Then there was the whole Little Red Ridinghood

thing, where he dressed in drag as Red's grandma and tried to eat her.

Of course, Red turned the tables and pounded on him 'til he was dead. That made her an instant folk hero around here until she had to flee the kingdom to avoid the vengeance of the other wolves. They even made an awesome horror movie about it that Gramps let me stay up and watch one night.

Sorry. I've gone on too long about them, but it's always good on Huff n Puff Day to remember that it's a celebration of a wolf-free life.

So—back to today—this was the first year trolls were allowed in the pie-eating contest. The honorable King Cheznott had found that the reason for us not being allowed—namely, that trolls with pie all over their mouths looked kind of gross—was unconstitutional. So my gramps wasn't going to miss this for the world.

ADMITTEDLY, KIND OF GROSS

MUNCH MUNCH

We were walking up the enormous driveway to the festival when I heard hooves clopping on the asphalt behind us. I turned and was excited to see it was my friend John "the Knoble Knight" Knoble.

HEY! ZARF AND FAMILY!!

"Great to see you guys!" John had been to our home a few times for some of my mom's famous mutton. Since "the Snuffweasel thing," he'd become almost like part of the family.

(A few months before, we had saved the kingdom from a bunch of seven-foot-tall rabid Snuffweasels. No biggie.)

GRR.

A woman leaned out from behind him to smile and wave, and it took me a moment to realize that it was no woman . . . it was my TEACHER! Miss Flett!

HI, ZARF!

I managed a stunned "Hi" and a quick wave of my paw. My friend John . . . and my teacher? What was this? A date? Teachers aren't part of the dating pool!

"We'll see you guys in there! And Zarf, I challenge you to at least one game of Wolf Toss." John gave me a big smile and a wink before urging his horse on up the drive.

My mom looked like she could just about pop with happiness. "That's your teacher Miss Flett, isn't it?"

My gramps chimed in. "Aye! I'll say it is. A foxy lass too."

GRAMPS!
GROSS!!

Miss Flett was my favorite teacher by a mile, but she still had all that . . . teacheriness. As we walked on up the drive, I tried to imagine her as an actual human—without the air of pop quizzes and red Sharpies about her—but I just couldn't quite do it.

My family stepped up to the festival entrance, and a big security ogre turned around. I saw that he was armed with a semiautomatic slingshot, probably on the off chance that an actual wolf would show up in town for the first time in a bazillion years. When he saw us, his big grin died on his face. He leaned in and sniffed at Gramps. "Thought I smelled a wolf, but it's just yer troll stench. Kinda odd, ain't it, the way wolves and trolls smell 'zackly the same."

OH, GREAT. TROLLS.

(I wish I could refute this, but it's true. One of the crueler tricks of nature is that the scent profile of trolls is pretty much identical to that of wolves.)

The ogre started chuckling. "You ask me, they shouldn't even allow trolls to Huff n Puff Day. Might give the kiddies nightmares!"

My gramps chuckled.

YE WON'T GET MY GOAT TODAY, SON.

"It's a day for celebratin' and eatin' and drinkin'.
So you'll pardon us as we 'ave at it."

We threw our shoulders back and walked by
holding our heads as high as we could.

My dad and Gramps made a beeline for the nearest
concession stand, and my mom caught me by the
shoulder.

"Remember what you promised me, Zarf. No
more getting into it with the prince. I can't stomach
having you tossed in that dungeon again, all right?"
She was still recovering from my last run-in with
His Highness.

I PROMISE! IF
I NEVER HAVE TO
TALK TO THE LITTLE
PHLEGM SACK, IT'LL
BE TOO SOON.

She gave me a lingering "mom stare" to show she meant it before ruffling my hair and letting me go.

I came around the corner to find the backyard jammed full of party-goers. My friend Kevin was off to the side by the huge koi pond, wringing his hooves over a long table full of overstuffed sandwiches.

Kevin is the vertically challenged son of Stan Littlepig (aka "the smart pig with the brick house"). The main thing you should know about Kevin is that when it comes to worrying, he's like that old Knight Service saying . . . he worries more before nine a.m. than most people do all day. What does he worry about? Doesn't matter. He's a professional fretter. It can be seventy-eight degrees and not a cloud in the sky, and he'll figure out an angle.

"Happy Huff n Puff Day, Kev!" I walked up and patted him on the back. He was sweatier than I expected, and almost shaking with anxiety.

"HAPPY? How can I be happy at a time like this??"

LOOK AT ALL OF THESE MAYONNAISE-BASED SANDWICHES!!

"It's a disaster waiting to happen, Zarf! Do you know what two things don't go well together? MAYO and DIRECT SUNLIGHT! If we don't do something soon, this party's gonna be a DIARRHEA-THON!"

Just then our friend Chester walked up, grabbed a greasy-looking tuna fish sandwich, and crammed the whole thing in his mouth.

HEY, ZARFSH.

Chester Flintwater (my Second-Best Friend—but it's really close) is the son of the Notswin court jester and next in line for the position when his dad steps down. That's gonna be a tough gig for a guy who may actually be missing his funny bone. Chester is to funny what those sad-eyed kennel dog commercials are to cheery. But he tries. Oh, does he try.

Let me be clear. These guys, Kevin and Chester, have my back and I have theirs. Despite their quirks, I wouldn't trade them for the world. As my gramps always says, "Ain't nothing wrong with a lil' weird."

"Hey, Chester." I kept talking as Kevin and I picked up the table and moved it a few feet over into the shade. I saw just a bit of the tension leave Kev's shoulders. "Did you see who John came with? I think he's on a date with Miss Flett!"

SERIOUSLY? Chester strained his neck to see over the crowd, and swallowed loudly. "Knoble Knight for the win! Miss Flett's the coolest!"

He was right. Miss Flett WAS the coolest—as teachers go.

Kevin was distracted, looking at the angle of the shadows from the house and judging how long the sandwiches would be in the somewhat cooler shade. "Maybe if I rigged a fan blowing over some ice . . ."

We hung out for a few minutes until Kevin got too fidgety and announced he was off to inspect the Dragon Dog water.

TEEMING CESSPOOLS OF BACTERIA IS WHAT THEY SHOULD CALL THEM IF THEY...

And just like that, he was off on another Kevin Mission.

I shrugged and grabbed a mufflebeast and Havarti wrap from the sandwich heap.

· 2 ·
ACCEPT NO SUBSTITUTES

STAY ON TARGET...

Chester and I were passing the Ferret Flip game when there was a high-pitched honking and a flurry of activity off to my right. People were scampering out of the way as a vehicle parted them like a herd of sheep.

AAAA!!

BEEP BEEP! CATERING EMERGENCY! MOVE IT OR LOSE IT!!

It was Goldie, also known as Miss Locks, the lunch lady, in a beat-up old golf cart with "Goldie's Catering" written on the side—and a giant fiberglass slice of pie attached to a spring on top. Goldie smiled when she saw us.

"Well, if it isn't Scruffy and Scruffier." She pulled up alongside us. "Hop in if you want, but be quick about it."

I jumped in beside her. Chester was still clambering onto a stack of coolers in the back when Goldie was rolling again.

"Is it the mayonnaise situation?" I asked, holding on tight to the edge of the flimsy roof. "Kev seems pretty worked up."

Goldie glanced at me sideways like I'd lost every marble in my head.

"The mayo will be fine. And tell Kevin to stop with all that talk. It's bad for business. No, what we have is a mutton shortage. On Huff n Puff Day, for cryin' out loud!!"

"Mutton shortage?" This was the first I'd heard of it.

"Yeah. Something's been getting at the livestock around the village. Stealing 'em. Eating 'em. I found prints in the mud that look like dog prints, but larger . . ." Her eyes shifted off to the woods, like she'd lost her train of thought for just a second. "But anyway, I'm comin' straight from a pickup on the docks. One thing this crowd won't be denied is their mutton."

I almost tumbled out of the cart as Goldie swerved wildly—narrowly avoiding taking out a gnome in a "Puff This!" T-shirt.

"So we're on a mutton mission?"

Goldie gave her head a shake. "Agh. I wish, Zarf. It's not mutton. It's Smutton."

My face smashed into the plastic windshield as Goldie slammed on the brakes. Chester did a somersault into the cart, ending up upside down between Goldie and me.

SMUTTON? YOU'RE KIDDING, RIGHT?

Smutton is maybe the nastiest of all of your artificial meats. It comes in a bright pink can, suspended in a gray, snot-like preservative. I wouldn't touch it on a dare.

"You're gonna try to pass off imitation mutton to these people?" I leaned in and whispered, "If they figure it out, they're gonna go nuts. Remember the Frogurt Riots?"

"Don't get yourself in a lather, Zarf. I have a hunch they won't notice the diff'rence. Trust old Goldie."

"People will know," I said. We got out and started unloading the coolers onto a big table near the Dunk-a-Wolf booth. "I'd know."

"That's funny." Goldie grunted, hefting the largest cooler onto her considerable shoulder. "I've seen you ask for seconds plenty of times in the cafeteria."

Chester and I froze. She walked off into the crowd, cackling. "Thanks for the help, guys! See ya at the fireworks!"

· 3 ·

ONE FOR
THE AGES

Chester and I were in line for the Dragon Swings of Death when I spotted Sierra through the crowd.

Okay, okay.

Let's get this over with. I've put off talking about Sierra for long enough, because, you know . . . girls and stuff. Yes, I like her a bit, but talking about it makes me want to stuff my head in a honey bog or something.

Yes, she's cute, but it's more than that. She's also cool. And smart. And funny. She hauls around this little homemade backpack everywhere she goes. She writes for the school blog and the yearbook, and her stuff is always great. But she's also . . . get this . . . nice to me. Why? I'm not entirely sure. Being of the troll persuasion, I'm always caught off guard by random kindness. It may be left over from when her family first moved to town. We were in second grade. I guess I was kind of decent to her on her first day—joked around a bit—and she's always remembered that. Or something. I can't read minds.

Chester nudged me with his elbow. "Hey, hey."

I nudged him back and murmured under my breath, "Don't call me that."

Just then she looked over and saw us. Her face lit up in a smile, and she waved.

Even here, she had that backpack. Apparently, she'd made it out of a beat-up old basket when she was little. It was kind of funny-looking—no question—but she took that basket-pack every-where. I'd seen her get razzed by the other girls about it, but she just kept on bringing it to school like it was her favorite thing in the world. You have to respect that kind of weird.

She was in line with her family for Flumpberry slushies. (Or Flumpshies, as they're called.) She started doing pantomimed poses like she was in a big hurry and all irritated, which cracked Chester and me up.

She was checking her watch and putting her fists on her hips all huffy and tapping her feet. She mimed loading a huge cannon and carefully aiming it at the people in front of her.

Her mom looked around, all smiles, to see who Sierra was joking around with. When she spotted me, a look of distaste slid across her face. She grabbed Sierra by the arm and gently turned her away.

She was leaning down to whisper something in Sierra's ear when a super-wide giant in a faded Prancing Knights jersey stepped between us, and the Sierra Show was over.

Either Chester hadn't seen what Sierra's mom did, or he pretended he hadn't for my sake.

I NEED TO DO MORE STUFF LIKE THAT IN MY ROUTINE.

"I might ask Sierra to ride the Ferris wheel during the fireworks," I blurted. It just came out all at once like that.

He wrinkled his nose for a second before nodding his head, the bells on his jester hat jingling. "Okay . . . I can see that."

Just then there was a loud, rude snort behind us. My stomach did a flip when I turned to find one of Prince Roquefort's bodyguard ogres standing inches away. (Not Buddy. He's the ogre that's kind of okay.) Let's call this one Jerky McOgreface.

PATHETIC.

He sneered at me in a way that made my troll blood give a little kick. How much had he heard?

We gave each other a minor stare-down before he pulled out his phone and started texting. "Sierra Scarlet and a troll," he chuckled. "Funniest thing I've heard in weeks."

At some point, we met back up with Kevin. He'd grabbed a frozen MuttonPop from somewhere that seemed to have been just the thing he needed to calm him down a bit.

Trust me, neither Chester nor I was going to tell him about the Smutton situation. A not-freaking-out Kevin is something to be cherished and encouraged.

He did tell us he'd gotten a "talking-to" from his dad about spooking the festival-goers about the food.

My gramps, thrilled to have the chance to compete, just barely lost the pie-eating contest to a nine-foot-tall ogre named Gut, but then fell asleep full and happy in a lawn chair by the corn dog trailer.

We rode most of the rides and played every game the festival had to offer. Our favorite, as usual, was the dunking-booth, where one of the carnival workers dressed up in a goofy-looking wolf costume. His sole job was to hurl insults at you until you could throw a bull's-eye pitch and put him in the water. Whoever had the job today was nailing the insult part of his job. Especially when Kevin stepped up with a fresh pile of baseballs.

Kevin stretched and cracked his knuckles. The sun was just ducking behind the hills, and all over the grounds, paper lanterns in the shape of straw, stick, and brick houses were being lit.

HEY, BACON BIT! GIMME YOUR BEST SHOT. LIL' PORK RIND!

Ordinarily I'd have worried that the short jokes were going to upset Kevin—he's super-sensitive about his height—but for several years, I'd seen just how much he enjoyed this booth. It seemed like the worse the insults, the better Kev's aim became. He just stood there and waited for his moment like some kind of Zen master.

Kevin took a deep breath, grabbed his first ball, and fired. He missed, but barely.

Kev fired a second shot that made a loud *ping* when it caught the edge of the metal bull's-eye. So close.

A small crowd had gathered as the insults kept coming. "I'm gonna Huff and Puff and make me a nice little ham sandwich, Short Stack!"

That was the one. With one smooth move, Kevin swept up a ball and nearly knocked that bull's-eye off its hinge. There was just enough time for the "wolf" to mutter a little "uh-oh" before he went into the tank with a huge splash. The crowd let out a cheer and Kevin got jostled around with pats on the back and congratulations.

Rebb Glumfort, an odd little wizard kid from our class, walked up to Kevin—his hair and robe looking like he'd just rolled out of bed—and patted him on the head. "That'll do, pig." Then he just walked away, in typical Weird Rebb fashion.

As we walked away from the booth, I heard the soaked guy in the wolf costume sputtering and laughing. "Nice shot, kid."

· 4 ·

BEST LAID PLANS

SHOWTIME!!

It was time for Chester's dad's comedy show. The three of us made our way to the front of the stage, jockeying for position with a couple of elves wearing shirts from Mr. Flintwater's comedy tour the year before.

First up, Stan Littlepig climbed the stairs and trotted over to the microphone.

HAPPY HUFF N PUFF DAY TO ONE AND ALL!! EXCEPT WOLVES, OBVIOUSLY!

He continued with his usual thanks and announcements, including a request for "No placing magic spells on the Port-o-Pottys, please. While it IS funny, it can also be a real bear to clean up."

Then he paused dramatically before introducing "The Jester of Jollies, the Clown with the Class—FESTER FLINTWATER!!"

A cheer went up as Mr. Flintwater did a goofy walk to center stage. He had the crowd in stitches before he even got to the microphone.

He started strong with a pie to the face that just killed. I mean, the man was a comedic genius. He took a pie in the face like Mozart—if Mozart had been a pie-in-the-face kind of guy.

The crowd was really getting jazzed up as Mr. Flintwater's set continued. Everybody knew what came next, and we were ready. Fireworks city! And the Littlepigs did not hold back on the boomers.

The Huff n Puff Day fireworks were legendary. They brought in Purple Pazzlers, Sizzling Willies,

Strawberry Stinger Bombs . . . Kevin told me they'd had a couple of New Guinean Eyebrow-Fryers flown in for the finale.

I spotted Sierra standing with her little sister and parents and started making my way through the crowd toward her. I got there just as Mr. Flintwater thanked the crowd and the applause swelled to an ear-splitting roar. She smiled when she saw me and gave me a fist bump.

I shoved my hands in my pockets and, looking off all casual-like, started asking her about riding the Ferris wheel.

There was a big squeal of feedback from the sound system . . . and it was followed by a voice.

THAT voice.

WELL, NOW. THIS IS FUN, ISN'T IT?

I'm not sure how to accurately get across my annoyance at having my most horrible of all horrible classmates, the prince, interrupt me at this moment. Imagine eating a bowl of cookies-and-cream ice cream. Then imagine with only a couple bites left you find half of a dead rat at the bottom. And then the ice cream–coated zombie half-rat sits up and hisses at you.

SSSSS

Yeah. That about describes the feeling.

But please, allow me to give the floor to His Majesticalness Prince Roquefort of Notswin.

"Loyal subjects! Please, please. Hold your applause. I know it's a thrill to see me, but we do have some sparklers to get to."

I slowly turned away from Sierra, aware that my mouth was hanging open.

THE ALWAYS FLATTERING "HALF-WIT FLY-CATCHER" LOOK.

"As many of you know, my father, your king, injured his rotator cuff last week during a rather heated croquet match. So I have come to the festival in his stead."

LUCKY YOU, AM I RIGHT?

"Then, just now . . . I got the most marvelous of ideas in my brain! Would you all like to know what I think this party needs?"

Ugh. He was just insufferable.

"A KING AND QUEEN OF HUFF N PUFF DAY!! Huh? RIGHT?" There was a general sound of approval from the crowd, followed by light applause. "That's why I'm naming your first-ever king and queen of the festival!"

The crowd was getting into it now as the little toad reached into his fancy coat pocket and pulled out a piece of parchment. He actually pulled out a little pair of reading glasses that I know he didn't need. "So, without further ado . . . your First-Ever King and Queen of the Huff n Puff Festival are . . ."

SIERRA SCARLET AND ZARF BELFORD!

The crowd applauded and went nuts—for about half a second. Then it was like they realized what he had said and the applause fizzled.

Wait . . . What? Had I misunderstood him?

Someone in the crowd shouted "A TROLL??" and someone else screamed "SERIOUSLY??" and I knew I'd heard right. I turned and saw the confused look on Sierra's face as someone behind me howled in confusion.

The crowd started some pretty serious murmuring, and a quick look of disgust flashed across Sierra's mom's face.

"Come on, you two! Get yourselves right on up here! Don't be shy!" Prince Roquefort was signaling for us to come up on the stage. I wondered if he'd had a stroke. Some kind of psychotic break with reality.

The surprised crowd began moving back to clear us a path to the stage. Every single face looked confused or stunned or angry—except for Chester, who jumped out into our path.

"Come on, you two! Woo-woo!" What Chester lacks in social graces, he makes up for in enthusiasm.

Sierra and I slowly walked up the steps to the stage. I caught bits and pieces of the mumbling around me. ". . . makes no sense at all . . ." ". . . smellier than a wet dog, and that hair . . ."

We walked across the stage to where the prince was waiting like a tiny game show host.

LADIES AND GENTLEMEN!

"Let's have a big round of applause for your new festival king and queen!!"

There was a smattering of applause (maybe my parents?) and more than a few boos, but I think the most common reaction was silence.

He went on. "Let me tell you what I'm thinking! I'm thinking the king and queen oughta take a nice, romantic ride in that big fancy Ferris wheel to watch the fireworks!"

HUH?? AM I RIGHT??

Wait. What? How could he know about . . . ? Then I looked over and noticed the prince's ogre from the Dragon Swings line standing at the edge of the stage, stifling a laugh in his huge paw.

The prince looked right at me and gave me a big ear-to-ear grin, but his eyes didn't match the rest of his face. They looked crazy, like little pits of evil.

I turned and saw Kevin in the crowd, wringing his hooves nervously.

KEVIN'S PATENTED "OH BOY, THIS IS BAD" LOOK.

"SO . . . Is this what you wanted, Zarf?" He turned and chuckled to the crowd, like he was in on a joke they hadn't quite caught up to yet.

"See, people . . . MY people . . . I'm just having a little fun here. I mean, OBVIOUSLY. Because this troll has himself . . ."

. . . A BIG OLD WHOPPER OF A CRUSH ON SIERRA!!

"He was going to ask her to ride the . . ." But he couldn't finish, as he dissolved into loud laughter.

I felt like somebody'd dropped a piano on my head. My face flushed, my knees buckled, and I had the immediate urge to run off into the woods and never look back.

Instead, I froze.

Roquefort was bent over laughing so hard, I hoped he might rupture something internally. I felt the blood rush to my cheeks and to the tips of my ears.

Now, you may wonder: Hey, Zarf? Isn't that the very same blood that makes you go into one of your trademark troll fits of murderous rage and snarling, spitting anger?

It is. But apparently on some subconscious level, Shame beats Anger—or at least it did this time.

The crowd had started laughing along with Roquefort—nervously at first, but it was gaining strength. He was wiping his eyes. "Ahhh . . . Ha-ha. Can you imagine?"

"Heh. Seriously, Zarf. You're just ridiculous. Now, get off the stage."

Suddenly his smile was gone. I hesitated for a moment, until I saw Jerky McOgreface coming across the stage for me, cracking his knuckles. Dazed, I went down the steps into the laughing crowd, wishing the stairs could keep going down into a big, Zarf-sized hole where I could curl up and die.

Avoiding Sierra's gaze, I chanced a look back up at the prince. He had slid up beside Sierra. "Let's get serious, now . . . Obviously, *I'm* your festival king."

I MEAN, DUH. AM I RIGHT?

The crowd started to applaud for real. This was an outcome people could wrap their brains around.

"So light those fireworks up over there! And I think it's only fitting if the REAL king and queen go take a ride on that big—"

And right then . . . that's when we heard it.

The first blood-curdling howl.

· 5 ·

BOOM

A wolf howl—there was really no mistaking it—pierced the noise of the crowd. It was clear, loud . . . and really close. I don't think there was a single living creature at that festival who didn't break out head to toe in goose bumps the size of railroad spikes.

Before the first howl died out, there was a second. And then a third and a fourth. The howls were all unique, with slightly different pitches and tones, like a nightmare version of a barbershop quartet. But they were all loud, and close enough that we felt them in our bones.

Everyone stood there like statues as the howls faded. Then the first of the fireworks exploded overhead. It was as if a starter gun had gone off to start a race—the crowd took off running at once. The result was total chaos. As the deafening explosions and flashes of light continued, people began slamming into one another like screaming pinballs.

The prince dropped the microphone and leaped into his ogre's arms—knocking Sierra backward. She stumbled over the mic chord and went down hard.

I was trying to hop onto the stage when I was slammed to the ground by a large cow-woman in a neon dress. Feet and hooves were pounding everywhere, so I tucked up in a ball and pulled my ears in so they wouldn't get stepped on. I was kicked and knocked around repeatedly until the crowd thinned a bit. I staggered to my feet and saw by the flickering light that Sierra was gone. As I turned to look for Kevin, I felt a large paw grab my arm. It was my dad, with my mom and Gramps close behind him.

ARE YOU OKAY? ARE YOU HURT?

I fell into step with them as we fought through the crowd, and another explosion shook the air around us. "I'm fine. But my friends . . ."

"Your friends will be fine, Zarf. We need to get our family home safe." I turned back and saw Kevin with his mom and little sister, Ima, bathed in pink and purple light, running away in the direction of their house. I looked back at my dad and nodded.

People were running everywhere as we made our way down the driveway. I almost tripped over a gnome waving a huge crossbow around and yelling into the night like a lunatic.

YOU WANNA PIECE OF ME, YOU HAIRY MANIACS??

The rest of our trip home was relatively uneventful until we reached the bridge over our house. We could hear the preprogrammed fireworks show winding down in the distance. That's when John came galloping up on his horse. His eyes were worried.

"Miss Flett? Have you seen her?" We all shook

our heads. His horse pranced around on the cobble-stones as John looked up and down the street. "I'm worried. She's not answering her phone either."

My dad stepped forward. "Can I help? We can organize a search party."

John turned his horse back around. "No. I've called on the knights. You all get inside and lock the doors."

I'M SURE SHE'LL TURN UP.

But he sure didn't look sure.

We all got inside, and my dad went around checking the downstairs doors and windows. It had been a rough night, so after seeing that everyone was okay, I headed up to my room. Now that some of the adrenaline was draining out of me, I felt like a big wet sack of troll guts and shame.

← ME

I flopped onto my bed and stared at the ceiling for a while. Maybe asleep I wouldn't feel so humiliated. As I shut off my light, there was a knock at the door. After a moment Gramps walked in, his hands in his pockets. He didn't say anything—just walked over to the window and checked the lock. Then he sighed and stood there looking out into the night.

Finally, he spoke, without turning around.

I slid down in the bed. "No."

He was quiet for a bit. "I always knew tha' prince lad was a turd, but wha' he pulled tonigh' was jus' . . ." Then his words just died off.

He found his way over in the dark and sat down on the edge of my bed. The springs groaned like they were in horrible pain, and I had to re-adjust so I didn't roll into him. We just sat there quietly for a bit.

"Hope so." I could feel him nodding. "I really do . . . and I'd imagine th' Knight Service'll have this all under control by first light. Bet she'll be right there where she belongs tomorrow. Givin' ya yer mornin' lessons."

He sat there long enough that I started to nod off, and then he patted my leg and grunted himself up from the bed. Before he slipped out the door, he spoke in a tired voice.

· 6 ·

MONDAY, MONDAY

The following morning was dark, drizzly, and cool, which suited my mood perfectly. I'd barely slept, and was hoping against hope that school would be canceled. Canceled forever would be good.

My gramps was still sleeping, but when I entered the kitchen I got an "Are you okay?" smile from my dad and a long hug from my mom. Is there a worse torture than having your parents feel sorry for you?

We all sat around the radio until official word came that school was still on for the day.

GROOOAN

The announcer said the Knight Service had been busy throughout the night and had found no trace of wolves. While citizens were told to stay vigilant, we were encouraged to continue on with our normal activities. The croquet tournament at the castle was back on, and the official word from the king was "Have a Nice Day."

There was no mention of Miss Flett, which I thought was odd, but I hoped that meant she had turned up.

Kevin was, of course, a nervous wreck—so his parents walked him as far as my house. My dad was heading out the door for the docks and stopped us before we left.

"Zarf. Kevin. I just want you to promise me you'll be on the lookout for anything odd. It sounds like everything's fine, but just . . . be careful."

Kevin jumped and twitched more on that walk to school than I've ever seen. He was like a Flotswinian Jumping Mushroom on Adderall.

But he was concerned with how I was doing, as well. "Are you okay?? I mean, that was *brutal* . . . No offense."

I sniffed and pulled my hood tighter. "I'm kind

of hoping the wolf scare knocked the whole Sierra thing right out of everyone's brains."

It hadn't.

As soon as we stepped in the front doors, someone let rip with a big whistle and a "HEY, LOVER BOY!"

I turned around and started to walk back out, but Kevin grabbed my sleeve and aimed me back into the school.

As I turned down the main hall, people were turning around to point. Sten Vinders made a big trumpet noise with his mouth and yelled at the top of his greasy jerk lungs. "Make way for the Fancy-Pants Festival King!"

There was a lot more of it—from Sten as well as some others—as I made my way to my locker. I just kept my head down and did my best to tune it out.

We met up with Chester, who tried to play it off like the whole thing hadn't been that bad.

I MEAN, SURE, THE WHOLE VILLAGE WAS THERE—BUT THOSE IN THE BACK COULD BARELY HEAR IT.

We walked into first period—Miss Flett's class: Fable-ometry—and the first person I saw was Sierra. Of course.

She looked up, blew a lock of hair out of her face, and gave me a quick embarrassed smile while she rummaged around in her backpack.

I needed to talk with her about what had happened, but not today. Today was about not dying from acute embarrassment.

The entire class was milling around. I heard someone talking about Miss Flett and realized word must have gotten out about her disappearing the night before.

Roquefort was sitting on his desk like he owned the place and blathering on to his ogre bodyguards and anyone else in the room.

"Was I afraid? Not for a second. I once killed three wolves, you know. With um . . . with only a toothpick." He was extra full of it this morning. "The wolves have a name for me in their world. Blosh . . . um . . . Bloshdwart."

Chester plopped into his desk and spoke up. Loudly.

"WHOO!" He leaned back and put his hands behind his head.

I tried to stifle a laugh—remembering my promise to my mom—but couldn't. I blurted a loud "Hah!"

Roquefort's head snapped around. Using one of the ogre's paws like a step stool, the prince climbed down from the desk while glaring at Chester.

KEEP TALKING, YOU DANCING MONKEY. KEEP LAUGHING.

Chester rolled his eyes, chuckling. "Okay, Bloshdwart."

Ignoring him, the prince turned to me as I settled into my seat. That evil grin was back. "I trust you had a lovely evening, Zarf."

Laughter rippled through the room. Anger started to well up from my feet, but just then the bell rang.

Everyone turned at the same time to look at the empty chair behind Miss Flett's desk. Miss Flett was never late. She usually blew into the classroom about three minutes before the bell on a cloud of

Xeroxed worksheets and spicefruit-scented perfume, but she had never been late. And we all knew it. Everyone found their seats quietly, and I heard Tina Squeegar quietly muttering "oh no oh no oh no" under her breath.

Five minutes later, the class was losing its collective mind. Everyone had moved their desks around and was whispering nervously in little groups. Kevin scootched his desk over to mine. There was a fine layer of sweat on his snout.

THIS IS BAD. THIS IS REALLY BAD.

"What if the wolves got her, Zarf?" He sat looking out the window for a few moments. "And . . . and if they didn't, we're supposed to have our test tomorrow, and I have literally a hundred and fifty questions to ask her before I do my studying!" (Kevin is the only person I know who studies up on how to study for a test. Pre-studying, he calls it. Huge eye roll.)

I was shocked. "How can you be worrying about a test?!"

MISS FLETT COULD BE DEAD!

Kevin looked horrified. "NO, NO! You don't understand! I'm SO worried that something happened to her. So much so that I can't even think that way or I'll have a panic attack! But then . . . if I pretend she's okay, then I start panicking about the test!! I'm . . . I'm in a panic spiral here, Zarf!"

Like I've said, the kid has made worrying an art form.

I CALL IT "AAAAUGGH IN BLUE."

A few minutes later, everyone clammed up as we heard footsteps coming our way. Our principal, Mr. Haggard, waddled in with a death grip on a to-go coffee from MotherGoose in one hand and the last bite of a jelly donut in the other. There was a small spot of what looked like jelly donut right in the middle of his stomach region. He looked stressed out and kind of sweaty.

OKAY. EVERYBODY SIMMER DOWN.

"We're unable to reach Miss Flett. That's not like her, so we're obviously concerned. We'll keep trying. We're in touch with the Knight Service, and we'll let you know as soon as we know anything."

I felt sick. I glanced over at Sierra, who looked stunned.

"I'm certain Miss Flett will show up, so in the meantime, we're all going to carry on with our day. Right?" Haggard looked around the room from student to student. He stuck the last of the donut in his mouth—clearly a stress eater—and wiped his sugary fingers on his khakis. "In a weird coincidence, we had a new substitute teacher stop in this morning looking for work. So . . . Y'know . . . That was convenient." He turned toward the door.

The class turned as one to see what the Substitute Lottery had brought us today.

At the risk of sounding like a jerk, Mr. Woolentail was odd. Profoundly so. His voice was high and nasally like he had a cold. And he was a sheep who just barely looked like a sheep. He had an elongated, wrinkly-looking muzzle and his tail looked all out of whack. Here's a drawing I did.

He just looked uncomfortable in his own skin—or in his own wool, in his case. It seemed to hang on him like a cheap suit.

Something about him made my paws itchy. That's a weird thing that happens to me when I get a bad feeling about things.

The sub spun around and pumped Principal Haggard's large hand enthusiastically.

Oh, no. We all quickly realized that this was a substitute of the Over-Eager variety. The kind that would clap his hooves together a lot and try to get us to think of him "less as a teacher and more as a pal."

As soon as Principal Haggard was gone, Woolentail hopped up and parked his big sheep butt on Miss Flett's desk.

"Listen, gang. I know some of you are a little concerned about your teacher. But she'll be fine, I'm sure. And I think we can really have some fun here! I want you to think of me less as a teacher and more as your pal."

· 7 ·

COUNTING
SHEEP

Mr. Woolentail insisted we go around the room and tell a bit about ourselves. This seemed like a huge pain, considering this guy would in all likelihood be a one-day sub. But we did it. He slowly circled the classroom as we talked, completely absorbed in our answers—filling the room with the smell of his oddly familiar cologne.

I won't make you suffer through the "Getting to Know You" exercise, but it was as awkward and soul crushing as you'd expect. The prince went last, and of course his "little bit about himself" lasted for ten minutes.

When that awfulness was done, Mr. Woolentail saw there were only a few minutes left in class. "Does anyone have any questions? I see Miss Flett has a test scheduled for tomorrow."

Kevin nearly launched out of his desk. "I actually have quite a few questions! Like, will it all be story problems? Will we be required to show our work? Is it multiple choice? How MANY choices? Will it include the material from chapter twenty-six? Will the Humpty Dumpty Theory be covered? Can I bring my inhaler?"

"Whoa, whoa, whoa!" Woolentail got up and strolled, smiling, over to Kevin.

SO MANY QUESTIONS FOR SUCH A LITTLE PIG.

Mr. Woolentail leaned down until he was right in front of Kevin's face. "Someone seems extra nervous about the exam. Perhaps I can help, friend-o."

Kevin looked a little uncomfortable. "Yeah?"

Mr. Woolentail suddenly straightened up and laughed. "I'll tell you what, Kevin. After school, I plan on staying around and doing some paperwork. I can take a look at the exam Miss Flett has in her folder.

So if you want to swing by after last period, I should be able to—"

He was interrupted by the bell. When it was done ringing, he looked back at Kevin. "How's that for a deal?"

Kevin collapsed back in his chair, relieved.

THANK YOU! PANIC HAS SOMEWHAT RELAXED ITS ICY GRIP ON MY POOR HEART.

I stuffed my books into my backpack, and by the time I looked back up, Sierra was out the door—which I guess was okay, since I wasn't sure what I'd say to her anyway.

As I left the room, Prince Roquefort slid by and patted me condescendingly on the back. "You really were hilarious last night, troll."

I couldn't help firing back at him. I remembered my promise, but it was like my voice had a mind of its own.

The prince froze. His smile disappeared and his little face started turning red. He got up in my face—or as close as he could, being about a foot tall.

"Did you just suggest that I eat butts?" His eyes narrowed. "ME?? The PRINCE of NOTSWIN??"

I clenched my teeth and fought back the urge to stuff his stupid little royal boots down his stupid little royal throat.

The prince pointed one tiny, gloved hand up at me. "You'll get yours, troll. Someday soon. And when that day comes, I'll be there watching and laughing. Enjoying it. With a tub of popcorn and a nice

big soda to wash it down while I take in the show."
Then he turned and stalked off down the hall.

I was fuming. I had to stand there rubbing my
ears and counting to ten, trying to get my troll anger
under control so long that I was late to my next class.

Something about that sub Mr. Woolentail wasn't
sitting right with me. He just seemed . . . unnatural.
It was like watching a bad actor in a movie, but I
couldn't put my finger on what was so off about
him. I was all lost in thought about this as I entered
the cafeteria for lunch. And the lunchroom at
Cotswin is one place where it doesn't pay to have
your head in the clouds.

I slammed face-first into one of the school's larger
giants—my nose taking
a sharp poke from his
studded belt.

While it felt to me like I'd walked into a brick wall, I don't think the big guy even realized I was there. But my collision hadn't gone unnoticed, as someone behind me (I think it was Sten Vinders) told someone else, "See? Trolls are clumsy in addition to being stupid and smelly." It was like they were discussing the properties of cumulus clouds or something.

FUME
FUME

I let out a low grumble as I clenched my paws and fought hard to not dive over the table at Sten. One good rule of school life is to avoid confrontation in rooms where there is access to pudding. Insults may hurt, but a well-aimed cup of tapioca can gum up your fur for the rest of the day.

I'd forgotten my lunch that morning, so I sulked over to the line for some of Goldie's porridge. As she slopped my tray, she leaned over the sneeze guard, looking serious.

She whispered, "I don't mind telling you I'm concerned."

I told her I thought she'd show up soon, but what did I know? Goldie just looked off and nodded a few times before moving to pour gruel on the next student's plate.

The fair maiden table was really cackling it up as I went by. Sounded like the post-festival gossip was flowing freely—I just hoped it wasn't about me or Sierra. I kept my head down as I passed the rugby table—they sounded like they were up to something, and it paid to stay off of their radar when possible.

I took my seat with Kevin and Chester at the end of the long back table. Chester had his face buried in a Knoble Knight comic book. Kevin looked up from gnawing on a dried piece of mutton.

HEY, Z. WANT SOME JERKY? MY MOM MADE EXTRA.

Generally, it was best to keep your fingers and toes away from the table when Kevin and mutton were near each other. So, for Kevin to make this offer, he had to be in a relatively good mood.

"You seem fairly chipper." I sat down and started emptying packets of sugar on my flavorless, gray government-issue porridge.

"Honestly? I'm still worried about Miss Flett, but I'm just so relieved about the test! I was all tied up in knots about it, but now Mr. Woolentail's gonna give me the inside scoop." Then he waggled his eyebrows hard enough to make his snout bob up and down.

I shoveled another scoop of gruel into my mouth. "That guy doesn't weird you out a little?"

Kevin sat back, looking surprised. Then he shook it off and grabbed another piece of jerky. "*Pssssh.* You're jealous."

Just then, there was a flash of light and a pop to my left. I turned to see Rebb Glumfort sitting a couple of seats down the table. He was by himself, which wasn't all that unusual. Even the other wizard kids found him a little odd—so we'd told him a while back he was welcome to park it at our weird little table when he needed to.

Rebb, sporting a massive case of bed head, was waving his magic wand over a Fazzle candy bar and a bowl of onion and cabbage soup. I hadn't even realized he was there. He leaned in and sniffed at the Fazzle bar.

"Looks like it's still a candy bar, Rebb." I realized with an inward groan it must be the start of Spell Month in the wizard classes, a thankfully limited period of time that everyone but the magically inclined students dreaded.

"That's precisely what one would think, wouldn't one, Zarf?" (This is how he talks, I swear.) "One's assumption would be wrong. I reversed their appearances. But do not be fooled by this magical tomfoolery! This"—he pointed at the candy bar—"is still a bowl of soup. And this"—he pointed at the soup—"is still very much a candy bar."

Almost glowing with pride, he broke off a piece of the Fazzle bar.

I don't usually eat science experiments, but that
Fazzle bar looked about a thousand times better
than my porridge. I popped it in my mouth and
immediately regretted it.

It WAS soup! It felt like a candy bar in my mouth,
but there was no mistaking that onion and cabbage
taste. It even smelled like soup.

Rebb was laughing. "The spell can exchange all
of the inherent physical properties except smell and
taste, for some reason. And it lasts for hours. All
due to the Copperfield Principle, of course, where
the subatomic magical quarks' effectiveness are
limited by an inverse system of . . ." And just like
that, I remembered why I don't spend more time
with wizards.

I was rinsing my mouth with my chocolate milk
when Kevin, who'd been watching intently, leaned
over.

· 8 ·

A BIT SLOW
ON THE UPTAKE

I'LL SEE YOU GUYS LATER!

After last period, Chester and I passed Kevin as he excitedly hurried down to Miss Flett's room to meet the sub. I had to admire the little nut job's study ethic.

I was kind of distracted as Chester and I made our way to the treehouse—my mind kept going back to that sub. His over-eagerness. His weird, misshapen body—all lumpy and awkward—like he was smuggling a bunch of elbows under his coat.

Chester tried out a new joke on me. He used me as a test audience a lot, much to my agony.

"Okay. Okay. How do you make a tissue dance?"

I cringed, wondering how bad the punch line would be.

I groaned and gave him a courtesy chuckle.

I think we were both avoiding talking about Miss Flett. Chester spent most of the walk telling me about a gnome in his English class whose parents had let him get a tattoo.

"Whose parents allow that? My dad would kill me—or take away my Benny Hill videos at the very least."

We were approaching the Wishing Tree, and I was doing my best to stay engaged in the conversation.

"It's like an eagle holding a big ugly wolf in its claws or something. But the thing is huge. It's maybe six inches tall. Six inches! His entire body is maybe twelve inches tall! The wolf barely fit!"

SWEET, RIGHT?

He was starting to go on, but he must have seen the blank look on my face. My entire body had gone cold. Something about that wolf tattoo had flipped a switch in my brain.

The wolf barely fit.

Big teeth.

Smells like Gramps.

Miss Flett missing.

We stood there at the base of the Wishing Tree in complete silence while all of the pieces fell into place in my brain.

"We have to get Kevin." I must have sounded like a robot. "We have to get him right now." Then I unfroze and took off running. Chester didn't hesitate, and in a moment was running at my side.

"What's the problem?" he shouted at me as we bobbed and weaved through someone's backyard trees, knocking the small branches out of our way.

Between my heart being in my throat and the running, it was hard to keep yelling. But I managed to get it out.

"I knew something wasn't right with that sheep! Think about it," I gasped. "The teeth! The smell! The way his clothes didn't fit him right! That wasn't a sheep, Chester. Mr. Woolentail is a wolf, and he's gotten himself alone with a Littlepig!"

Chester's eyes grew wide.

He put his head down and ran even faster.

As we came flying across the Cotswin school parking lot, Goldie was out front washing the windshield on her Grub-Mobile. She looked up, startled, as Chester and I started yelling.

"Call anybody! Kevin's in trouble! WOLF!"

And then we were past her. The entrance door banged open and echoed like a cannon in the empty halls as we dashed for the stairwell. We took the stairs four at a time and careened off the poster-covered wall at the bottom. I could see the door to Miss Flett's room was closed. My heart, which had been lodged at the back of my throat, dropped into my feet.

Chester reached the door a hair before me and threw it open. We tumbled into the room in a cloud of sweat and fur and panic . . . and probably some BO, I'll admit. We were pretty ripe by then.

Kevin looked up. He was sitting at his usual desk, calmly making notes. He looked mildly confused. "Hey, guys."

I was so out of breath, I could hardly speak.

"Mr. Woolentail" was casually leaning against Miss Flett's desk.

HEY, HEY! LOOK WHO IT IS!

"Did you guys decide you need some help with the ol' studyin' as well?" He stood up and walked behind the desk. "I was givin' my good buddy Kev some pointers, and he was telling me a bit more about some of your classmates."

"Kevin," I said, as calmly as my heaving chest allowed. "I need you to go stand by Chester." Woolentail flinched as I took a few steps toward him.

Kevin just sat there. "You guys have no idea how much help Mr. Woolentail is being. He's—"

I jumped onto a chair, grabbed the top of Woolentail's head and yanked. A hood pulled back, revealing a startled, mangy-looking wolf.

Kevin started screaming in a higher pitch than I thought he could.

AAAAAAA!!! YOU'VE TORN HIS SKIN OFF!!

But Kevin's scream died in his throat as he saw the wolf's darting eyes go from stunned to furious in a flash.

"BACK OFF, TROLL!!" He jerked away from me. "I'll tear yer mangy throat out 'fore you can raise yer paws." And now that I was face-to-face with a wolf for the first time in my life, I believed him.

He went on, and I noticed that high nasally voice

hadn't been part of his act. "So ya caught on. Well BRA-freakin'-VO, Scooby-Doo." Then he yelled over his shoulder to the windows.

Chester and I fell for his trick and looked out the windows—there were no other wolves out there. But that was all the time the wolf needed. In a wickedly smooth move, he swept Kevin up under his arm and was out the door of the classroom.

Chester and I hit the hallway at a sprint. Kevin was squealing in a way that I hoped would bring out other teachers or Principal Haggard, but the building seemed as good as empty.

We followed them up the stairs and down the main hallway. We had to catch him before the front doors. We were gaining on them when we passed the overflowing trash cans outside the cafeteria—

where Chester stepped on a half-empty carton of Porridge-in-a-Box.

He slid a good twelve feet—a move that would have been worthy of applause under any other circumstances—and smashed into one of the trophy cases by the front alcove. The entire case came down on him in a crash of jousting and archery trophies. I spun to see if he was okay as the wolf and Kevin pounded through the main doors. Chester was trapped under the heavy case. He'd had the wind knocked out of him and his ankle had been smashed pretty good, but he was frantically waving me on.

GO! GO! I'M FINE! GO GET OUR PIG!

· 9 ·

CHASING
THEIR TAILS

I slammed my way out of the front doors and my heart sank. The wolf, with Kevin squirming like a fish under his arm, was all hunched up on a stupid little electric Gnome-Ped and getting away fast. Or as fast as one can on a tiny electric gnome bike.

Had the wolf brought a Gnome-Ped? Stepping over the discarded sheep costume, I spun around to look for a bike or something when I spotted the Grub-Mobile. Goldie was nowhere in sight—I thought she was probably in the office getting Principal Haggard—and the little key was in the ignition.

I swerved onto the sidewalk with the gas pedal floored. I could hear the spring from that giant pie sign skreenking around like crazy, and hoped that pie wasn't heavy enough to pull the cart over.

SKREENKA
SKREENKA

GOLDIE'S
CATERING

Kevin and the wolf were a little ahead of me, but I felt like I could catch them. I was yelling at the golf cart and urging it to move faster.

I will admit that a chase between a golf cart and a Gnome-Ped lacks some of the dramatic elements of a Hollywood blockbuster. It doesn't have the pulse-pounding soundtrack, or the roaring engines, or the explosions . . . or the speed, for that matter. What it does have is the quiet whir of the electric motors, the annoying sound of the pie sign creaking back and forth, and the clank of a few cans of Smutton rolling around the floor of the cart. But my heart was pounding plenty.

I felt that oh-so-familiar angry troll blood pumping its way into my brain, and I let it keep right on pumping.

I was right behind them as they pulled onto the main street. A family of elves had to step out of their way, into the street. They seemed more irritated than alarmed, until they realized it was a wolf at the wheel. Then they lost their ever-elven minds.

The wolf looked back and I saw my chance. I reached around the windshield and grabbed on to Kevin's curly tail. I pulled and it stretched out farther than I expected.

I slowed down, hoping Kevin would pop out from under the wolf's arm like a cork. But the wolf must have had a tight grip, 'cause Kevin just shouted louder.

Then my paw slipped and Kevin's tail popped free with a loud POINK sound. They pulled ahead again. I gunned the engine and slowly started pulling up beside them as we passed the candlestick maker's shop. Stunned faces were flashing by in the windows. I readied myself and crammed a large Smutton can between the gas pedal and the bottom of the dashboard. Then, feeling like Indiana Jones and a flying squirrel all rolled up into one, I jumped.

I landed on the wolf's back like a spider monkey. He let out a startled yelp and started reaching back and swatting at me as we zipped past the butcher shop. I heard Goldie's cart crash into something behind me, but I just squeezed my eyes shut and clung to him like a cheap sweater. The Gnome-Ped started swerving around the sidewalk, forcing a business-gnome to dive for cover in a big ceramic planter.

I got an arm over the wolf's eyes and pulled back as hard as I could. The Gnome-Ped swerved to the left and dropped off of the curb. The wolf overcorrected— and we went hurtling straight through the huge front window of the Notswin Bakery.

We were lucky in that the baker, Mr. Schmidt, had opened the windows that day in hopes that the smell of baked goods would draw in customers. We were not lucky in that the front window was also displaying an array of sticky cinnamon rolls, pies, pastries, and one of the largest wedding cakes Mr. Schmidt had ever baked.

The masterpiece didn't stand a chance. It exploded as we blasted through it.

The three of us landed on the store floor covered in cake, under a shower of pastries and pie filling. As soon as Kevin landed, he scrambled—hooves slipping in icing and cake—out of the wolf's grasp.

Mr. Schmidt and a handful of customers hurried out of the store—even faster once they got a look at the angry wolf wiping custard out of his seething eyes.

The wolf kicked out with his hind leg and drilled me hard in the chin. Then he was going after Kevin, again, growling. "Come here, ya little bacon-flavored Snausage!"

Kevin squealed and backed up as far as he could against a counter, kicking at the wolf's paw. There was nowhere to go. He grabbed a squished hot cross bun off of the floor and chucked it at the wolf's head.

Ignoring the icing in my nose and the ringing in my ears, I grabbed a heavy cookie sheet and stepped up behind the wolf.

Just as the wolf got a grip on Kevin's ankle, I reared back—angry troll blood surging through my body—and smashed him so hard, they heard it two kingdoms away.

CLAAAANG!!

· 10 ·

WE HAVE WAYS OF MAKING YOU TALK

I slid across the floor to Kevin, who was tucked up in a little ball and looked like he might lose his sanity at any moment.

"You okay? Are you hurt, Kev?"

I realized he was starting to shake. I grabbed him by the shoulders and got right in his face. "It's okay now. Everything's okay." I looked at the pastry-splattered chaos around us. "I mean . . . relatively speaking."

Kevin looked up at me, and I could tell he wasn't all there. His brain must have been firing at about ten percent.

"...but I'm pretty sure that was a wolf," he whispered.

I couldn't help but laugh. "Oh, you think?"

Kev leaned out slightly to look behind me at the unconscious wolf.

"I'm . . ." It was actually kind of heartbreaking to see him coming to terms with being face-to-face with his worst nightmare. "I'm pretty sure I'm going to pass out now."

And he did.

Goldie, the Knoble Knight, and a limping Chester showed up a few minutes later. By that time,

Kevin was coming around and I had tightly bound the unconscious wolf in an entire roll of baker's twine. Mr. Schmidt was over in the corner, noisily lamenting the demise of his huge cake.

'TWAS MY SWEET, SWEET MONA LISA, SHE WAS.

Goldie rushed in and gave Kevin and me bear hugs as I launched into an apology.

GOLDIE! I'M SORRY I TOOK YOUR GOLF CART! I DIDN'T KNOW WHAT ELSE TO DO! I WAS...

She smiled and put a stubby finger against my icing-covered lips. "Zarf, Zarf, Zarf. Shut yer cake hole. The Grub-Mobile will ride again."

John gave me a hearty pat on the back. "You did great, Zarf. You did really great." He squatted down between Kevin and me.

NOW TELL ME EVERYTHING.

So, between Kevin and Chester and me, we did. It took a while, and Mr. Schmidt got us glasses of ice water and a plate of huge, castle-shaped pastries before he went back to cleaning up the colossal mess we had made. At one point, the wolf came to and started making demands.

HARASSMENT! UNLAWFUL IMPRISONMENT!! I DEMAND TO SEE MY LAWYER!

John walked over and casually shoved a wadded-up apron in the wolf's mouth and told us to continue.

The sun was starting to set when we finished our story. John had a grim look on his face.

"I hope I'm wrong, but I'd imagine this wolf knows the whereabouts of Miss Flett." He turned and glared at the wolf, who glared right back. "I think it's time for some answers."

Chester made a rude noise with his mouth.

PFFFF! LIKE HE'LL TELL US ANYTHING.

A strange grin slid across the knight's face. "Oh, there are things we can do to get a wolf to cooperate."

AREN'T THERE, WOLFIE?

* * *

Three minutes later, we had the wolf up on a well-used butcher block under a bright kitchen light.

John turned to address us. "Okay. This may not be pretty, but we're going to get answers." We all nodded solemnly.

LITTLE-KNOWN FACT. WOLVES HATE BEING TICKLED. I MEAN HATE IT.

He reached over and yanked the apron out of the wolf's mouth, who immediately started growling and cursing at us.

"Just try it!!" The wolf was aiming his hate right at John. "Tickle me and lose a finger at the very least! Maybe a hand! I have the bite power of fourteen Snuffweas—"

But right then John stepped up and put the tips of his fingers against the bottom of the wolf's bound feet—right on that ticklish fur that sticks out between the pads. That shut the wolf up. "Ground rules: You so much as nip at any of us, we tickle you harder. Got it? Shall we begin? Let's start with your name."

The wolf's eyes were darting between his feet and the knight. "NEVER!"

I'LL NEVER TELL YOU A SINGLE...

John fluttered the wolf's back paw fur. "Tickle, tickle."

Immediately the wolf broke into loud, agonized laughter. "HAA-HAA-HAAAAA! All right, all right! HA-HA! Stop! I'm the Awkward Awful Wolf!!"

The knight stopped and smiled. "Not quite the Big Bad Wolf, huh?"

The wolf was trying to regain his composure. "Listen, little knight." He paused, out of breath from the laughing jag. "There will only ever be one

Big Bad Wolf. How dare you even say His Name!"
John started up the tickling again.

HAHAHA! THERE'S A... A STORM COMING! HAHAHA! AND YOU'RE TOO LATE TO DO HAHA ANYTHING!

Then he peed a little from laughing, which didn't make Mr. Schmidt very happy.

THAT'S WHERE I ROLL THE PIE CRUSTS.

I'll spare you the rest of the interrogation. A crowd had gathered in the front window, so if you want gory details, I'm sure there are some gossips that'll tell you the whole thing.

At one point, it seemed like the wolf was getting

used to the tickling. This didn't faze John, who had apparently done this kind of thing before.

"Mr. Schmidt? I know you make savory pastries here as well. Do you by any chance have any . . . BLUE CHEESE?"

The reaction from the wolf was unbelievable.

Mr. Schmidt went to his fridge and came back with a huge tub marked "BLUE CHEESE— EXTRA SMELLY," while John just smiled, watching the wolf squirm around.

"Little-known Fact Number Two: Blue cheese skeeves wolves right the heck out. It's like their Kryptonite."

The wolf went nuts as John took the lid off the tub. "Don't you get that—rrretch!—stuff anywhere— GAGGG!—near me!!"

All John had to do was wave a spoonful of that cheese under the wolf's nose and he was telling us everything we needed to know.

WHY DID YOU TAKE MISS FLETT?

"To get the subsititute gig!" The wolf retched loudly. "To get to the students."

Chester stepped up. "To get Kevin? Revenge against the Littlepigs? Why didn't you just sneak in and grab Kevin at the festival?"

The wolf rolled his eyes and looked at Chester like he was addressing an idiot. "It's not about the stupid pigs, brainless. He just put himself out there on a platter! He was telling me all about his—gag—classmates. And I mean, sure—taking out a Little-pig would have been a juicy little bonus—but it was all about getting our paws on Red Ridinghood's stupid kid."

That shut us all up.

"Come again?" John asked as he grabbed the wolf's chin, prepared to wipe blue cheese on his upper lip. "Red Ridinghood never had a kid, and if she did, why would she live here? Last I heard, Red left the country . . . and I don't think she ever stepped foot in Cotswin."

The wolf tried halfheartedly to jerk his chin away. "Like you all don't know. Like it isn't the best-kept secret in the kingdom."

We all stood there looking at one another for a few moments, confused.

The wolf looked around at us, amused. "Wait. You honestly didn't know? That's HILARIOUS!"

John started in with the tickling, and the wolf started talking again.

"Look, look. Here's the deal. Th' one thing we know fer sure is that Red Ridinghood's kid lives here. Attends Cotswin. And we WILL have our revenge for what her mother, Red, did to Big Bad. Remember the storm I said was coming? It's a wolf storm, okay? Big ol' storm of wolves, comin' at ya. It's not gonna stop—and you're not gettin' your precious Miss Flett back—'til you hand over the Ridinghood child."

I'll never forget the look on John's face as he leaned over the wolf. It was a glare that could have melted glass. He scooped up a handful of cheese and prepared to shove it into the wolf's muzzle.

OKAY, RODENT.

"This is where you tell me where they have Miss Flett—or you're gonna be smellin' blue to the end of your days."

"Whatevs." The wolf just smiled and turned his head. But three seconds later, you could have heard his cheese-muffled screams from three blocks away.

· 11 ·

MALICE IN CHAINS

Things wound down quickly after that. The Royal Ogre Guard showed up in their horse-drawn paddy wagon to arrest the wolf. For once in my life, I found the ogres' thuggish ways kind of entertaining as they shackled the criminal, manhandled him out of the shop, and tossed him like a bag full of rotten turnips into the back of the wagon. The gathered crowd was cheering and yelling wolf-related insults the whole time.

John was all business, barking out orders into his phone. Within minutes, several of his best men had assembled in front of the bakery with the knight's trusted steed. His suit of armor was disassembled and hanging off of the side of the saddle.

He mounted his horse and backed up to where Kevin and Chester and I were standing by the curb.

He smiled, but it didn't really reach his eyes. He looked off down the darkened main street. His horse was pawing at the ground, ready to get going.

"I'm gonna go get your teacher. I'd tell you all

to stay out of trouble, but I know you guys. So just promise me you'll be careful. It sounds like this may not be over."

Chester sniffed loudly and hiked up his pants.

DON'T YOU WORRY, JOHN-O.

"Any more wolves come around here, they'll have to get through 'The Chester-ster.'" He looked a little awkward when he realized adding a "ster" to the end of his name didn't really work.

I tried to help him out. "The Chesternator?"

Chester sniffed and looked away sheepishly. "That'll work, I guess."

The knight leaned down closer. "Listen. As far as I'm concerned, you're all Deputy Knights until I get back. I want you on high alert."

Then he straightened up, yelled to his men, and they galloped off in a cloud of dust.

While Kevin let out a high-pitched whimper,

Chester fist-pumped and did an awkward little jump for joy on his one good foot.

"That's the raddest thing I've ever heard!" I wasn't sure when the term *rad* had come back into popularity, but I knew this was a big moment for Chester, so I let it slide.

Goldie pulled up in her banged-up Grub-Mobile and told us all to pile in and she'd give us rides home. Chester said he had a ride and limped over to hop onto the back bumper of the paddy wagon as it left for the castle.

When we got to Littlepig Manor, the rides and booths from the festival were still set up, looking kind of spooky in the dark. Kevin mumbled that the high school volunteers wouldn't be back to tear everything down until the following weekend.

"And don't ask about playing the games or bringing Sierra over for a Ferris wheel ride or anything. My folks won't even let me play with the stuff." Kevin slid out of the cart like an old man, looking sad and tired. "See you tomorrow, guys."

As Goldie pulled away down the driveway, I could feel her looking at me. I tried my best to ignore her.

I sank down in my seat. "Goldie, I am not in the mood."

COTSWIN ABUZZ

When I got home that night, my family had just heard about the whole thing. My mom was in what can only be described as a *tizzy*. (Her word, not mine.) I could tell she'd been crying from the pile of wadded-up Kleenex in her lap. My mom goes through Kleenex like other people go through oxygen.

My dad and Gramps were pretty upset as well, but at one point, when my mom wasn't looking, Gramps elbowed me in the side and gave me a quick thumbs-up.

WAY TA GO, WOLFCRUSHER.

The next morning, Kevin wasn't his usual frantic self—he was almost like a robot whose circuits had finally overloaded.

TOO FREAKED OUT TO COMPUTE.

It looked like he hadn't slept, and he barely raised an eyebrow when my mom gave him a couple of mutton cakes to put in his lunch.

We were about a block from my house when Kevin

said something—but barely. He spoke so quietly, I almost didn't hear him.

THANK YOU, ZARF.

Then I saw his face and realized he was really upset. His eyes were all glassy with tears. "Oh! Hey! What's . . . Are you okay?"

Kevin sniffed and looked away. "No. I'm really not." He took a few deep breaths.

I'M SUCH A WORRYWART SPAZZ-OUT WUSS!

"What?" I stopped.

It all came flooding out at once. "My folks were already all tweaked that I freaked people out about the festival food and then had to sleep with the lights on 'cause of the wolves and the test and then I get taken by a wolf and I'm such a wimp I need

saving and I squealed the whole way through town
and Meredith the Meat Girl probably saw me and
I'm embarrassed and I don't even want to go back
to school where people are gonna look at me like a
little baby and point and stuff." Then he took an
enormous breath.

YOU'VE GOTTA BE KIDDING ME!

I reached over and punched him in the arm. You
survived a run-in with a WOLF, Kevin."

Kevin pulled out his handkerchief and blew his
snout. "It's not like it was the Big Bad Wolf."

That got me laughing. "Well, that's a good thing,
him being dead and all."

Kevin started walking again. "Look, it's just . . .
my dad and my uncles faced the worst wolf ever. I
face one Awkward Awful Wolf and I fall apart. It's
humiliating."

"Kevin." I stopped him again. "You came up

against a wolf—doesn't matter what wolf—and you're ALIVE! That's amazing!"

Kevin just kicked at a pebble with his hoof.

He mumbled something under his breath.

"I'm not moving 'til you say it, Kev. Now, who's the pig?"

Kevin looked off to the side. "I'm the pig."

I punched him on the arm again. "Louder."

Kevin looked up and a weak grin slid over his face. "I'm the pig!"

"Darn right you are." With that taken care of, I gave Kev a friendly push and we started walking again.

The janitor, Mr. Heffernan, was standing in the bushes cleaning the cafeteria windows, and gave us a shout when we he saw us coming across the field.

HERE THEY COME! WOLF PATROL!

"If it ain't the men of the hour. You guys're the talk of the school! That and the whole Ridinghood thing, of course."

He told us there was going to be an assembly in the gym during second period to discuss the events of the night before. It was probably a good thing too, because once we walked through the front door, we could feel the jittery energy in the air . . . like the entire school was hopped up on energy drinks.

April Jeffries, a pig cellist in the orchestra, ran over as soon as she saw Kevin. She swept him up in a big hug and said how glad she was that he was okay. Kevin seemed to be too stunned to react other than letting out a little sound somewhere between a grunt and a whimper.

She let him go and looked over at me, and I could see in her eyes she wasn't sure what to do. I honestly think she was happy for me, but hugging a troll was out of the question. She pointed at me awkwardly.

"And you . . . Um . . ."

Then she scrambled away like she'd survived an encounter with a festering Sewer Mutant.

Just then the front doors slammed open behind us. I turned to see the silhouette of someone standing there in the bright doorway, fists on hips. It wasn't until he sauntered in a few steps that I realized it was Chester, wearing aviator sunglasses and a homemade "Deputy Knight" T-shirt.

My eyes rolled so hard, I almost fell over.

Chester sauntered up and pointed a finger gun at one of the Cheer-Maidens gossiping in the corner. "How you doin', ma'am?"

She looked at him like she smelled something bad before walking away. "Whatevs, clown."

Chester winked at us over the top of his glasses.

LADIES LOVE A MAN IN UNIFORM.

The first part of first period was kind of a blur. The office administrator, Miss Poodle, was acting as our substitute teacher—and wasn't really making any effort to control us. She told us that the test was canceled.

OBVIOUSLY.

I watched as Kevin almost fell out of his chair with relief.

All anyone could talk about was wolves and Ridinghoods and Miss Flett—until the PA system started to crackle. There was some amplified fumbling before a nervous metallic voice rang out.

WILL KEVIN LITTLEPIG PLEASE REPORT TO THE OFFICE FOR...UM...AN URGENT MESSAGE? VERY URGENT?

I turned around and Kevin's face was in the early stages of a Kevin meltdown. His snout was flushed and starting to twitch around. His ears were standing up straight and I swear there was a low hum coming off of him.

On a good day, a trip to the restroom can be a hyperventilating-worthy ordeal for Kevin. Getting called urgently to the principal's office was likely to put him in the hospital.

MEDICALLY SPEAKING, HE FREAKED THE HECK OUT.

"It's fine, Kev. I'm sure they just want to check in with you." I grabbed his arm firmly, hoping it would calm him down. "To make sure you're not gonna turn into a werewolf or sue them or anything."

Kevin just swallowed loudly, stood up, and stumbled out of the room like a zombie.

I got concerned when first period ended and Kevin hadn't returned.

I was looking for the little guy everywhere as we were all herded like cattle into the gymnasium.

As Chester and I shuffled in, he got a number of pats on the back for his part in the wolf chase, while I got a "Musta got lucky" and a shake of the head from one of the grungier-looking eighth-grade orcs.

Chester and I climbed to the top of the rickety bleachers and slid into a row. I was craning my neck looking for Kev, and sat on a half-invisible gnome wizard. (Man, I hate Spell Month.) He was disgruntled, to say the least.

Calling the crowd restless would be a huge understatement. It was like there was a school-wide Ants-in-Pants epidemic.

Principal Haggard waddled out to a microphone at center court—one of his loafers squeaking with every step.

"Good morning, Prancing Knights." Even from this distance I could tell he was sweaty and nervous.

"I'm sure most of you have heard about the whole substitute wolf thing last night. As well as the rescue mission the knights have embarked on to retrieve our beloved Miss Flett from the wolves at

Snuff's Pillow." He kept his eyes glued to the court in front of him as he let out a long sigh.

"I want you to know that I hold myself responsible for yesterday's events. I allowed a wolf into our midst, and I blame no one but myself . . . You all have my sincere apologies."

Wow. THIS was awkward.

"Well." He paused again. "I'm afraid I have more bad news. Very bad, actually."

For once in this school you could have heard a pin drop.

"At eight o'clock this morning, just as you were settling into your first class, the unthinkable happened." The principal paused and rubbed one of his big ink-stained hands over his face. "A large pack of wolves attacked Littlepig Manor. They have taken control of the home and everyone in it."

My stomach dropped as the gym exploded in whispering and murmuring. I was on my feet and fighting my way out of the row as the principal started shouting for everyone to be quiet. Some elf girl from my social studies class screamed.

"Please, everyone! Please! I know this is frightening, but please stay calm." He went on talking about the extra safety precautions that were being taken and blah blah blah, but I barely heard him. When I reached the bottom of the bleachers, Mr. Hirsch stopped me—as well as Chester, who was right behind me.

Mr. Hirsch grabbed us both by the arms. He had a powerful grip for a social studies teacher. "Kevin's in the office. He's fine. Let's hear what the principal has to say."

Mr. Haggard was now yelling to be heard over the gym full of panicked students. "Listen! Please! The authorities are at the house, and they are in communication with the wolf pack. They have heard the wolves' demands—ridiculous as they may be."

The room quieted as he let that sink in.

"The wolves are demanding that the son or daughter of Red Ridinghood, who they claim attends this very school, be turned over to them." His voice even got a little louder, and you could tell he was angry.

NOW, LET ME MAKE ONE THING ABSOLUTELY CLEAR...

He cleared his throat and crossed his arms defiantly. "No child of Little Red Ridinghood attends this school. The wolves are WRONG, plain and simple.

If there was a Ridinghood attending this school, I can assure you with every fiber of my being that I would be the first person to know about—"

"It's me, Principal Haggard!"

Time stopped. I knew that voice.

She was in the second row.

Shoulders back, head held high. Defiant.

Sierra.

·13·

BOMBSHELL

Everyone stared, stunned. Principal Haggard's mouth was hanging open so wide, he could have caught a lot more than flies.

"Wha . . . ? I . . . ? Sierra, please, I . . ." He was so flustered, he couldn't form a sentence. "I'm not sure what you're trying to . . ."

"It's okay, Principal Haggard. No one knows. My mother went to great lengths to make sure of that."

My brain was quickly connecting the dots. Sierra

Scarlet. The basket purse. Could that be from her mom's basket? The famous one?

The principal's flytrap was hanging open for business again.

The entire student body looked like it had been hit with a Freeze Spell—myself included.

Sierra went on in a voice so calm it was eerie. "The woman you know of as my mom is my aunt— my mom's sister. My mom had to . . . had to leave. The wolves were after her and she had to flee the kingdom." She paused like she was swallowing some pretty heavy emotion. "I've kept the secret the way my mom said it had to be . . . but there's no way I'm going to stay quiet if it puts innocent people—or pigs—in danger." She stepped through the students in front of her to the gym floor.

For three seconds, no one moved. I could hear my voice saying "No. No. No." I'm still not sure if it was out loud or if I said it to myself.

The gym suddenly erupted. There were people yelling NOOO! and people yelling TURN HER OVER! and all sorts of unprintable things, all at once.

Much like the crowd, I was upset, angry, worried, confused (and maybe a little hungry) all at the same time. It was too much, and I felt like my brain was going to explode.

CAUTION:
EXPLODIN'
TROLL BRAINS

The gym was going nuts. Everyone was shouting at once, and I saw at least two elves pass out (as they tend to do). Principal Haggard swept over and put a protective arm around Sierra, moving her swiftly toward the exit, all the time yelling into the microphone.

"Okay, students! We'll sort this business out—

ha-ha! Assembly over! Carry on! Back to class! Nothing to see here." He dropped the microphone and signaled Mr. Hirsch, indicating we should follow.

The gym looked like a minor riot as we shuffled out. For reasons I don't fully understand, people were throwing paper and pens and pre-packaged snack foods. I remember seeing a small gnome hanging from the edge of the bleachers as I dodged a gruntberry granola bar.

Sixty seconds later, we were following Sierra and Principal Haggard into the office. Sierra was explaining something about her mom not wanting her to live a life on the run. The principal looked like he'd aged twenty years in the last few minutes. But I was most concerned by my quick look around the office. There was no sign of Kevin.

"Where is he?" I yelled as I continued to look

behind doors and under lamps. (I'm well aware
Kevin couldn't fit under a lamp, but desperate times
make you do some stupid stuff.)

It took Principal Haggard some effort to turn his
attention away from Sierra. "It's . . . What? He's
right over . . ." He turned and looked at the couch,
and his face fell even further. "He was right there!
With a pack of ice! He fainted and I . . ."

I was suddenly furious. All that practice at
controlling my troll anger went right up in smoke.

The principal was really sweating now. "There was the assembly! And he was . . . out cold, and . . . And don't take this the wrong way, but I locked him in here. For his own good! So he didn't try to run home and do something stup—" He froze. We all followed his line of sight to the open window above the couch. It had sweaty little hoof prints on the glass.

With about two bobs and one weave, Sierra, Chester, and I were past Principal Haggard and Mr. Hirsch and out the door of the office, out the front doors, and flying across the field at top speed. Haggard and Hirsch tried to catch us, but Mr. Haggard wasn't exactly in great shape and it was well known that Mr. Hirsch had a bad hoof from an old minotauring accident.

As we bolted across the Carousel Street bridge that passed over my house (yeah, yeah—the trolls live under a bridge—let's move on) I managed to huff out a quick question. "So . . . is your name even . . . Sierra?"

It took her a second to time her breathing so she could answer, but she managed a sideways glance at me—sort of a "Seriously? Is this important now?" look.

"It's Sierra."

I glanced over at Chester, who was gasping and panting like a Wheezing Bush—but not slowing down in the least.

We turned to cut through the woods to Kevin's house, which slowed us down a bit. As we came up the hill, we saw them. Knight Service trailers and wagons and—more alarmingly—SQUAT team tents lined the top of the ridge.

I should probably explain. The SQUAT team is an elite group of volunteer, highly skilled, crime-fighting archers. It actually stands for Super-Qualified Uniformed Archery Team. (I never understood why they needed the word *Uniformed* in their name. I mean, if you had eyes you could see they were in uniforms—but whatever. I guess they needed the U in there or they'd be the SQAT team, and then nobody'd know how to pronounce it.)

Seeing those SQUAT tents was alarming. I could only remember seeing the SQUAT team once before—when a Steam Dragon with a stomach bug tried to bathe in the town's fresh water supply—and knew they only came out when the situation was really serious. We were almost to the tents when there was a loud amplified squawk and some ear-piercing feedback.

"STOP!!" A large SQUATist (I kid you not, that's what they prefer to be called) with a bullhorn in front of their face stepped out of the closest tent.

The sinister voice was so deep and booming that it brought us all to a screeching halt. "WHERE DO YOU THINK YOU'RE . . . WAIT . . ."

The figure lowered the horn and started fumbling with the volume knob—revealing that it was Miss Locks. I had no idea she was on the SQUAT team, but I'd learned that Goldie was full of surprises.

She chucked the bullhorn back into the tent. "That stupid piece of crap has been acting up all morning. Makes me sound like Darth Vader running a drive-thru window."

She motioned for us to follow her up the hill. "You're here 'cause of Kevin."

Still catching my breath, I nodded. "Please tell me you got to him before he did anything stupid."

We reached the top of the ridge, where we could see Littlepig Manor in the valley below.

·14·

SUPER IN TENTS

WHAT DOES THAT MEAN?

Goldie sighed. "It means the little nut job got past us. We had just gotten here when he showed up. He went squealing down that hill and straight in the front door. 'Wee wee wee' the whole way. There was no way to stop him."

"So what happened?" Chester sounded frantic. "Is he okay?"

Goldie reached into her side pack and pulled out a canteen, which she handed us to pass around. "No

idea. It's been completely silent since he went in."
She grabbed a pair of binoculars hanging on a tree
beside her and handed them to me.

I focused in on Kevin's house, which looked
eerily quiet in the midday haze. There were maybe
a dozen motorcycles parked in the front yard. The
only other difference I could see was a big white
sheet hanging between two of the upstairs windows.
It had a huge paw print painted on it.

"What's with the paw?" I asked as I handed the binoculars to Sierra.

"That's what this pack calls themselves."

Goldie rolled her eyes and started over to a nearby table where two other SQUATists and a knight were looking over a big map. "Seems like The Claw would have instilled more fear, but maybe that's harder to draw or something."

She was showing us on the map how a perimeter had been set up surrounding the house, when Sierra stepped up and set the binoculars down.

Goldie looked up at her, confused. She glanced at Chester and me and back to Sierra. "Did I miss something?"

Sierra smiled in a kind of sad, lopsided way. "Kinda. My real name is Sierra Ridinghood."

One of Goldie's eyebrows shot up. She tipped her head sideways for a moment, looking at Sierra through new eyes.

Just then we heard a tiny electronic engine whining and straining up the hill behind us. We turned around and saw Principal Haggard hunched over the dented little Gnome-Ped from the night before.

He rolled up beside us and got (awkwardly) off of the ridiculous little bike. As he straightened his shirt and picked a few gnats off of his forehead, he looked up at us sheepishly.

"Yeah, it's mine. I won the stupid thing at the Huff n Puff raffle, all right? No judging."

Goldie invited us into the main tent, along with the lead knight and head SQUATist—Jack Horner (who'd come a long way since his corner-sitting, thumb-plum-eating younger days). What followed was a heated discussion, with Sierra insisting she be allowed to turn herself over—and the rest of us trying to convince her she was out of her flippin' mind.

We'd gone back and forth over this about thirty times when SQUATist Horner reached in his pocket and pulled out a Fazzle bar. My first thought, as he tore open the wrapper and took a huge bite, was that it was kind of rude. My second thought was that I hoped his Fazzle didn't taste like onion and cabbage soup. My third thought was that I had an idea.

I stood up. "Wait, wait, wait." Everyone turned. I was pacing now, trying to work this out in my head.

My troll brain isn't used to having big ideas, so it was a bit like blowing Play-Doh through a drinking straw.

"We all agree that if Sierra goes in, she'll instantly be Wolf Kibble, right?"

Everyone nodded.

LIKE DELIVERING THEM A BIG, SIERRA-SIZED PIZZA.

I paced a couple more lengths of the tent. "But we need to know what's happening in there, right? We need someone on the inside?"

More nods. Jack nodded and spoke through a mouth full of Fazzle. "That'd be great."

"So . . ." I was really pushing the limits of troll thinking here. "What if we sent in a wolf?"

Everyone was looking at me like there was something hanging out of my nose. Goldie just looked confused. "What? Like the Awkward Awful one? What possible good would that do? No way would he work with us."

I stopped pacing. "What if the wolf wasn't really a wolf?"

WHAT IF IT JUST LOOKED AND SMELLED LIKE ONE?

· 15 ·

HUNGRY LIKE
THE WOLF

Twenty minutes later, Goldie and I rolled up in front of the school with a very disgruntled wolf in tow. I mean, he wasn't even slightly gruntled. We lifted him off the back of the cart and forced him down the halls to the science wing.

It hadn't taken long for me to convince the group in the tent of my plan. If it worked with soup and a candy bar, it could work with a wolf and a troll, right? Right?

NO, SERIOUSLY.
I'M ASKING.

Everyone agreed that if we were going to do it, I was the only choice. After all, the Interchange Spell didn't change smells. So my lifelong burden of smelling like a wolf might finally pay off.

We hoped.

So we didn't freak the entire school out, Goldie and I stopped and shoved the protesting wolf into my locker (which still smelled faintly of Stink Dragon— long story) for safekeeping.

UNFAIR TREATMENT!
INHUMANE! AND IT...
IT REALLY, REALLY
STINKS IN HERE!

We knocked quickly and walked right into Mr. Jorgenspiel's fifth-period wizard class—and were shocked when a rather large swan woman—writing her name on the chalkboard—turned around to greet us.

She explained that this was her first day substituting for Mr. Jorgenspiel, who had gone to Wallen to tend to his aunt who was having surgery for an ingrown toenail. Gross.

Of all days for him to be gone! My heart sank until I spotted Rebb Glumfort, slumped low at his desk in the back row.

Goldie locked the doors to the cafeteria, flipped off the fluorescents, and pulled the blinds. After wiping some dried juice and a smashed Tater Tot off one of the tables, Goldie and I laid the Awkward Awful Wolf across it and tied him down. Then we turned to an extremely nervous Rebb. "What next?"

UMMMM... WE NEED TO TIE YOU DOWN TOO.

I hadn't counted on this, but Rebb explained that we both needed to be completely still for the switch to take place. So after getting wrapped up in some rope, I climbed up and tentatively lay down, shoulder to shoulder with the wolf. He'd been locked up in a cell all night with no shower, so he still smelled a bit like spoiled bakery goods.

YOU STINK.

THANKS FOR THE UPDATE.

The wolf was really irritated, but I think he would have lost his mind if he knew what was coming.

As Rebb stood up on the bench so he was looking down on us, I started realizing the full magnitude of what we were doing.

"Rebb, this is temporary. Right?"

"Should be. Supposed to last eight or ten hours if you do it right."

"Are you doing it right?"

"I hope so."

"Will it hurt?"

"No idea. The Fazzle bar didn't mention it."

Rebb took a last look at his notes before hiking up the back of his wizard robe and stuffing them in his pocket. With a shaking finger, he pushed his Coke-bottle glasses up his nose and took a deep breath.

LET'S DO THIS THING.

As soon as Rebb started waving his wand around, the wolf went nuts. "Wait. What're you doin', nerd? Get this Merlin fan boy away from me!!"

I looked over at Goldie, who gave me a nervous smile. Rebb started mumbling something that sounded like "gunter glieben glauchen globen" or something. When little sparks started floating from the end of his wand, I squeezed my eyes shut and held my breath.

It happened remarkably fast. The first thing I felt was a tugging at my paws and a tingle all over my scalp. Then there was a feeling a little like going over that first big drop on a roller coaster. My heart started beating faster and I was sweating, but I kept my eyes squeezed tight. Finally, it felt like the temperature in the room dropped and there was a sensation like . . . well . . . like I popped. Like a balloon popping. It didn't really hurt. It just felt . . . weird.

And then I heard Goldie gasp.

·16·

CH-CH-CH-CHANGES

The first thing I saw when I opened my eyes was the fluorescent light directly above me. Then I noticed the snout.

Imagine suddenly having a foot-long submarine sandwich where your nose used to be. It was disorienting. I turned my head to the side and there, just beyond the snout was . . . me. Zarf. Looking back at me with eyes that were getting wider and wider.

How can I describe looking over and seeing my own face screaming back at me? How can I describe looking down and seeing big gnarly wolf claws in place of my paws? How can I go on with this story without confusing you to death?

As soon as I assured her it was me inside the wolf body, Goldie untied me.

"Are you okay? Did it hurt? How do you feel?"

I sat up and stretched. I took a second to feel my long muzzle and my ears. I ran a finger along the point of one of my new fangs and was surprised

when I almost drew blood. Then I looked up at
Goldie and sort of laughed.

At that point, the wolf caught on to what had
happened.

"I'm a TROLL? SERIOUSLY?? A FILTHY
BRIDGE TROLL? Make me something else!
Please?"

Goldie and I thanked Rebb, who was now eyeing
me and keeping at least two tables between us. He
headed back to class and I spent a few minutes
clicking around the cafeteria getting used to my new

body. As soon as I could move around without holding the wall, we were back in the cart and headed for Littlepig Manor.

When we got there, the others were suitably impressed, and more than a little nervous around me—despite my constant assurances that it was me. Chester was beside himself with envy and demanded a few selfies. I insisted this wasn't the time or place, but he wouldn't shut up 'til I gave in.

We were heading to the main tent to work out our plan when we heard footsteps in the brush behind us. We all spun around just as my good buddy the prince and his ogre bodyguards (Buddy and the other one) stepped out from behind a mungberry bush.

The prince was *all* ticked off. "What is the meaning of trying to set up a defense against these beasts without ME, the bravest warrior in all of the . . . ?" Then Roquefort got one look at me and froze. All color drained from his face and he made a little squeak.

Before I had a moment to react, both of his ogres were flying through the air at me like airborne dump trucks. They slammed into me hard enough to knock my toenails off, and we went sprawling across the leafy ground into the base of a tree.

Everyone was yelling at once as Buddy was rearing back for a roundhouse punch. I just barely got my wolf mouth to bark out a few words.

Buddy paused for just a second. But it was enough. Sierra dashed in, grabbing his huge arm. "It's okay, Buddy! It's not a wolf! It's Zarf."

Buddy turned and looked at the prince, who was visibly shaking and looking around the group from face to face. "Whaaa?"

"It's true, Your Highness," Goldie said as she stepped forward—swallowing the word *Highness* a bit like it pained her to say it. "We had a spell put on him."

The prince started over toward me. I went to sit up a bit and he stopped. "That's Zarf." He was trying to wrap his tiny little brain around the idea. Buddy slowly lowered his arm.

I rolled my eyes as I slid over to lean against a tree. "It's me, Your Slow-on-the-Uptake-ness. Can we move on with this?"

That convinced him. He walked up to me and sniffed. "Well, isn't that just . . . *disgusting.*" He laughed his little hyena laugh.

LIKE A HORRIBLE, SMELLY WOLF WITH A GOOEY TROLL CENTER.

"I knew all the time, of course. I was just test-
ing my simpleminded guards here." Buddy grunted
quietly as his eyes met mine and he helped me to
my feet.

The plan, when it was revealed, was a bit less than
pleasing to the prince.

"SEND A STUPID TROLL IN?!?" He threw
his arms up and started pacing around the map
table. Everyone else tried to quiet him down. The
last thing we needed was for the wolves to get wind
of our next move.

"Prince Roquefort!" Goldie hissed. "You need to
keep your voice down, so . . ."

"YOU HAVE A PRINCE HERE, AND YOU
EXPECT A . . . A COMMON VERMIN TO
DO A DELICATE JOB LIKE INFILTRATING
THE—"

Goldie was furious. "Be quiet! You'll put Zarf and all of the rest of us in serious . . ." She tried to grab the prince by one of his flailing arms, but he squirmed away.

"WOULD YOU ASK A RAT TO TAKE OUT YOUR APPENDIX IF YOU—"

Goldie acted so fast, I almost missed it. She grabbed an empty teapot from the center of the table and tossed it at the prince.

Acting purely on reflex, he caught it—as Goldie reached into her shirt and pulled out Rebb's wand. (When had she grabbed that?!) She pointed it at the prince and muttered "Gunter glieben glauchen globen."

There was a bright flash of light and a pop before the prince dropped unconscious to the ground next to the teapot. We all stood there stunned. After

what seemed like an eternity, a small sound came
from the end of the teapot's spout.

...GROOOAANN...

Goldie went over and gently picked up the pot,
setting it back on the map. "Sorry, Your Highness,
but that had to be done."

The teapot shivered and suddenly jerked upright.

"Wait a second! What have you done to me??"
The spout curled down and felt the bowl part of the
pot, like a little elephant trunk.

"I'm . . . wait a second . . . I'm . . ."

I'M A LITTLE
TEAPOT!!
SHORT AND
STOUT!!!

He was still yelling, but it was so much quieter
and sort of tinny—like it was coming from a tiny

little speaker. I looked over at Sierra, who had both of her hands over her mouth. I was thinking she was upset until she finally broke and barked out a loud, relieved laugh.

Goldie looked around sheepishly at all of us. "It was all I could think of. He was putting us all in danger." She smiled nervously at the prince's bodyguards.

Buddy looked down at the teapot, now furiously hopping around the table, before shrugging his shoulders.

I stared at Goldie with my mouth hanging open (again). "How did you do that spell? I thought only magically inclined people could—"

Goldie cut me off. "I have no clue, Zarf. I just heard Rebb do it before and thought it was worth a shot."

I gave her a suspicious look and she just chuckled, patted me on the back, and walked away. "Honestly, Zarf. No idea."

It was decided I'd go in at dusk. Jack Horner wired a small microphone into the fur of my wrist so they could hear what was happening in the house. They gave me a tiny earphone that fit way down inside my ear so I could hear them as well. Finally, we all fell quiet as we waited for the dark—all except for the prince, but Goldie had thrown a blanket over him to muffle him even further.

We were watching as a couple of lights came on in the mansion.

YOU'RE GOING TO BE CAREFUL...RIGHT, ZARF?

"You betcha." I was trying to breathe slowly and keep myself calm, but it wasn't working. Because, you know . . . wolves.

When it was time, here's how we did it. On the count of three, I shot out of the woods and took off down the hill like I was being chased. The SQUAT team, hidden in the trees, started yelling and making all kinds of noise as I went screaming down the hill.

Goldie and the others let loose with a few carefully aimed arrows to make it look like they were close on my heels. As I heard a couple of them whizz past my head, I didn't have to fake my panic. "OPEN UP!! INCOMING!!!"

When I was maybe twenty feet from the front door, it swung open. A couple of arrows thunked into the side of the house as I crossed the last few feet and dove into the house.

The enormous door slammed shut behind me and I was in.

For better or worse, I was in.

· 17 ·

DEN OF THIEVES

Lying on my back, an expensive Oriental rug bunched up underneath me, I slowly opened my eyes. Three of my worst nightmares were staring down at me—all glistening teeth and curled claws.

One reached out and held a huge paw in front of me. "We thought you was dead, Awful!" I grabbed the paw and was helped up.

I glanced around at the group quickly. In a stroke of luck, each of them was wearing a battered leather jacket with their names stitched above the chest pockets—Horrible Hideous, Dangerous Deadly, and Sinister Sneaky. I wondered for a split second which one had done their embroidery.

I swallowed hard and forced a chuckle. Then I tried to mimick that high-pitched, nasal voice of Awkward's. "Shoooot. You kiddin' me? I was jus' toyin' with 'em. Bidin' my time ta git away."

"Yeah, right!" Horrible Hideous let out an awful laugh and slapped me on the back so hard I almost swallowed my tongue. He put a big arm around me and led me into the Littlepigs' home like he owned the place.

The tour was a short one. He showed me the guard posts—one watching out the front window, the other out the back window.

We swung by the dining room, where he pulled a leather jacket off the chair. As he helped me slip into it, I saw the name Awkward Awful stitched on the front. I'll admit that in spite of being completely terrified, I stopped for a moment to notice how cool that jacket was. It was like someone had captured coolness in its raw form and made a coat out of it.

After that we stopped in the kitchen, where he ooh'd and ahh'd about the size and contents of the fridge. "Flumploaf! Guacamole! Liverwurst!"

As he cracked open a Black Cherry Whizz, I heard Chester in my earpiece talking with the group in the woods. "It's true. Those pigs love some soda. I don't know how they have any teeth left."

Horrible drained the can in one gulp as he led me into the TV room, where he crumpled it and dropped it on the floor. "Lookit that flat-screen! That thing's bigger'n the front door!" I was a little distracted by the eight or ten rough-looking wolves lounging on the Littlepigs' furniture.

Huge clawed feet were all over the coffee table. Coasters were not being used. One of the wolves belched loudly and threw a bottle at the TV—currently showing some kind of cooking show. This resulted in a loud, fang-baring shouting match that left my knees shaking a bit.

GO BACK TO CASTLE CRASHERS!!

"Get bent! They're doing pork ribs in the next segment!"

I tried to make sure the gang on the hill was getting all of this.

"Boy . . . Look at all these wolves lounging in the Littlepigs' TV room!" I said, a little too loud, aiming my voice toward my wrist.

Horrible Hideous gave me a funny sideways look that lasted a little too long for my taste.

YEAH . . . I HAVE EYES.

Clearly I needed to be more subtle with my reports.

"Hey!" He slapped his paws together. "Wanna see the hostages?"

I gave my best fake sinister laugh as we started out of the kitchen. "Heck yeah I do!"

I heard Goldie in my ear. "Here we go."

As he led me up the stairs, Horrible explained the situation. "Now, unfortunately, we ain't allowed to eat any of 'em, yet. Boss says that's for after we get the Ridinghood brat."

I was flooded with relief. It sounded like they were all okay—at least so far.

We turned down a familiar hallway and saw another wolf sitting guard outside a familiar door— Kevin's bedroom. His jacket identified him as the Mad Malicious Wolf.

"Hey, Awkward! I thought you was dead or in jail!" He stood up and cuffed me on the ear hard enough that I saw stars. "Wanna see the scared little piggies?" Then he started making a snorting noise as he turned around and opened the bedroom door.

I stepped inside and my heart broke.

Kevin and his whole family were there, huddled up on the bottom bunk of Kevin's bed. His mom, his dad . . . and his little sister, Ima.

They were all staring at us, terrified, as we walked in the door. Kevin's eyes went wide when he saw me—or who he thought I was. "YOU!! How did you get out of—?"

I cut him off before he could bring up any more awkward questions. "SILENCE, PORK!"

Wow, it felt awful to yell something like that at

Kev, but I had to keep up the illusion. He clammed up, and he and his sister cowered, shaking. It made me feel so bad, I thought I might barf.

Horrible stepped into the room. He snarled and bared his teeth a bit, getting a kick out of the response this got. Then—and this was weird—he started singing and doing a happy little dance in front of the Littlepigs.

As he went on, Ima turned and buried her face into Kevin's chest. I was trying to catch Kevin's eye—maybe I could will him to see the me inside my eyes—when something shifted on the top bunk and I realized there was someone up there in the shadows.

It was Miss Flett. Wait. Miss Flett? How could she be here and at Snuff's Pillow at the same time? Were there two of her??

The wolf stopped his dancing and reared back, laughing. "That's my name, toots!"

I heard Goldie in my earpiece yelling to her fellow SQUATists. "Miss Flett is in the house!! The Snuff's Pillow story was a lie to lure our knights out of town!"

I had to admit that made more sense than the Miss-Flett-being-cloned theory I'd been forming.

Horrible stopped dancing and grabbed me by the back of the neck. "Let's get you up to see the boss. He'll be glad to see you in one piece."

But I had an idea. With Horrible behind me, I looked Kevin right in the eyes. He was peeking over a pillow, so I had to work fast before he hid his face again.

"Say, Horrible. You know if these pigs got any FAZZLE BARS?" And when I said "Fazzle bars," I pointed at my chest.

I COULD SURE GO FOR A FAZZLE BAR!

I said it too loud and patted my chest. Kevin's eyes looked a little confused, like he wasn't sure what was happening.

Horrible Hideous was pulling at me. "I don't know, man. We'll check."

I stood my ground, staring at Kev. "I don't want some disgusting CABBAGE AND ONION SOUP, y'know? No FLUMPLOAF. I want me a FAZZLE BAR!" I pointed like crazy at myself on the words *Fazzle bar.*

Kevin's eyes were darting back and forth.

This is something he does when he's thinking really hard—making connections in his brain. He also does it when he needs to go to the bathroom really bad, but I didn't think that was the situation this time.

Suddenly his eyes got huge. Something had clicked. But the look of wonder quickly turned to terror.

THAT WOLF ATE ZARF!!

"ZARF'S SPIRIT IS IN ITS STOMACH AND HE'S TRYING TO COMMUNICATE WITH ME!!"

Dang. So close.

But then the wolf yanked me out of the room. "Man, what is it with you and Fazzle bars? Jeesh. They're tasty. You like 'em. We get it." He was leading me farther down the darkened hall. "Now let's go let Big Bad know you're okay."

It took a second for my troll brain to absorb that.

WAIT... WHAT?

Did he just say what I thought he said?

Then I heard Chester screaming in my ear— "JUMPIN' SWAMPFROGS! The Big Bad Wolf is ALIVE!!"—and I was pretty sure I'd heard right.

· 18 ·

WHO'S AFRAID...?

When we stopped in front of the large door to the Littlepigs' bedroom, my heart was beating so loud, I was worried Horrible Hideous could hear it.

Goldie and Chester were whispering in my ear for me to breathe slowly and stay calm, which was only making me more nervous.

The door opened a few inches to reveal a short wolf looking up at us with suspicious eyes.

'S UP?

When he got a better look at me the small wolf opened the door to the room and let me in, leaving Horrible behind. The first thing I noticed was the haze of cigar smoke. The bed looked as if every throw pillow in the home had been brought up to make a nest for a large, important someone. The lights were dimmed and trays piled with food had been set up all over—but fortunately the bed/nest was empty.

"He's in here." The small wolf—Alert Attentive, according to his jacket—started toward the door in the corner, where I heard a slosh of water.

Attentive let me into the large bathroom and my heart stopped. There, surrounded by bubbles in the Littlepigs' enormous in-floor Jacuzzi tub, was

. . . The Boogeyman. The Terror. The one we tell campfire stories about. Alive and well and chomping on a huge cigar.

The Big. Bad. Wolf. How was he alive??

I've never had to fight harder to not turn and run in my life. Imagine finding yourself face-to-face with Dracula and a giant grizzly bear all rolled into one. That'll give you some idea how I felt.

He was larger and more terrifying than I had ever imagined. His left eye was covered in a dirty-looking patch and a good part of his right ear was missing.

Big Bad squinted at me with his one good eye and then started to chuckle. A cold sound so deep and rumbling, it made the floor shiver under my paws.

"So you're alive after all." He stubbed his cigar out on the tile floor. "We thought you got your idiot head shot off."

I realized I was supposed to speak. "Umm. Nope. No. Not dead. I'm . . . alive. Here I am. Livin'. Breathin'. All that."

I was babbling like an idiot. But Big Bad just chuckled again. "Awkward and Awful as always." He snapped his fingers. "Hand me a towel."

I turned around and grabbed one of the big monogrammed towels off of the rack and tossed it to him. He snatched it out of the air with an enormous paw and started to stand up out of the bubbles. He signaled for me to turn around, which I was more than happy to do.

"I don't suppose . . . and I know this a long shot here . . . that you got any info on the Ridinghood brat like you were supposed to, did you?"

I took a small step toward the door. "Well . . . not exactly. I . . ."

NOT ACCEPTABLE!

Big Bad shouted and brought his fist down so hard he broke the marble countertop, put a crack in the wall mirror, and made one of the faucets start running. I whispered as quietly as I could into my wrist mic, "You getting this?" and was surprised by how quivery my voice came out. I heard Goldie assure me they were getting every word.

I realized my whole body was shaking and my wolf tail had involuntarily curled up between my legs—like Chester's dog Pudding when he knows he's in trouble. I couldn't control the stupid thing.

I listened closely as Big Bad put on his jeans and slid into his enormous leather jacket. When he put his arm around me, I nearly jumped out the window.

"Awkward . . ." he started in a syrupy-sweet tone.

CAN I CALL
YOU AWKWARD?

I nodded, afraid to look up.

"Have you seen my eye? And my ear? I mean, have I ever given you an up-close and personal look at that Ridinghood girl's handiwork?

I had no idea if he had or hadn't, so I stayed quiet. I knew I didn't particularly WANT to see it.

"No? Well, listen. This isn't a game to me, Awk. I'm gonna call you Awk now." The sweetness had dropped back out of his voice. We were walking through the bedroom toward the door. "So, I don't know how this is going to happen, but . . ." He swung open the bedroom door and shoved me into the hallway. "You're gonna have to PROVE to me that you're WORTHY of being in this gang . . ." He suddenly crossed the hall and smashed me against the wall by my throat so I couldn't breathe.

He held me there—my breath cut off—as he huffed and puffed in my face for what felt like forever. His stare was so intense, I had to squeeze my eyes shut.

Then he let go. I slumped to the floor as he crossed back into the bedroom and slammed the door. My head was pounding and I was seeing stars as I gulped in air. I don't think I actually passed out, but I was close as I sat there listening to Chester in my earpiece.

· 19 ·

INSIDE TROLL

I was about to answer when I realized someone was standing over me. I looked up to find
Horrible standing there with a big cheese-eating
grin on his face.

I tried to pull my wits together as quickly as I could. "He wasn't too happy." I got slowly to my feet.

"Is he ever?" Horrible laughed and started toward the stairs. "Come on. We're going to talk about shifts. And you look like you could use a can of Flumpfruit Splash."

After a short stop in the kitchen, we headed into the dining room, where most of the wolves had gathered. The table was littered with playing cards, overfilled ashtrays, and a range of soda and beer cans. They were arguing over who should take which shifts.

I, on the other hand, was trying to figure out how to drink a soda with this long muzzle. I kept going to put the can to where my troll mouth would be, and ended up with Flumpfruit Splash down my neck. Then when I got it to my lips, it just felt un-natural. It was like using a burrito for a straw.

SIP.

The voices in the room were getting louder. A couple of wolves were snarling and gnashing their teeth about having to take the night shift when I realized I'd better pipe up.

"I . . . I'll take th' night shift watchin' them hostages. I don't mind none."

The whole room stopped and looked at me. Then at one another. Then a few of them started laughing.

OH, NOW THAT'S RICH.

"And then we come up in the morning to find you in an empty room all stuffed full of pig meat." It was the one called Sinister Sneaky. "They call me Sneaky and even I wouldn't trust *you* watching the henhouse."

There was more laughter, but I kept on trying. "Ha. No, no. I know my reputation. But as you all prolly heard, Big Bad ain't too pleased with me right now." This at least got their attention. "He says I need to prove m'self."

One of the dirtier, mangier-looking wolves in the corner chimed in. "Look. If doofus wants ta take that night shift, I ain't gonna complain none. I need my beauty rest."

Y'KNOW WHAT I'M SAYIN'?

He let loose with a way-too-loud, wheezy laugh—like this was the funniest thing anybody'd ever said, ever—that broke the other wolves up. There were high fives and "I hear that!"'s all around, along with some loud belches and lots of back slapping.

Most of the wolves had crashed for the night when I took my post outside Kevin's room at midnight. The wolf before me handed me the key and took his book with him, but there was a stack of Mrs. Little-pig's *Fairytale Inquirer*s beside the chair. I picked one up and tried to look like I was reading it while I listened and waited for the house to go quiet.

Chester chose this time to try and tell me a few jokes to help calm me down. It took everything I had not to beg him not to.

"Okay, Zarf. What do you call an alligator wearing a vest?"

AN INVESTIGATOR!

They got worse from there.

Around one o'clock I heard the downstairs TV shut off, and twenty minutes later the house was silent, other than some pretty impressive snoring from down the hall. I forced myself to wait another half an hour until I put down my magazine and turned to the door.

I'd thought about how I could get in there without Kevin and the others (okay, mostly Kevin) taking one look at me and squealing bloody murder. They'd wake every wolf in the place.

I got down on the floor and cupped my paw by the opening at the bottom. Then I whispered as loud as I thought I could.

I listened for a minute but didn't hear a response. "Kevin!" I put my ear to the crack and thought I heard some rustling around in there. "If somebody's hearing me, it's Zarf. Get Kevin."

There was more moving around and some whispering. Then the light in the room went on and I could tell someone was on the other side of the door.

"Kevin?"

"Hey, Kev. It's me. I'm gonna get you guys out of here."

There was a long pause. "You don't really sound like Zarf."

I sighed. "Well, that's the thing. I don't look like him either. That was me in there earlier."

I explained about the switch. We went back and forth a few times, as my worrywart of a friend was having a hard time trusting me.

Time was slipping by, and I was getting frustrated. And my wolf knees were starting to hurt.

Kevin's whisper came back from under the door. "Okay. Tell me something only you and I know."

Listen. I was under a lot of pressure. I had no choice.

"YOU POOPED YOUR PANTS DURING OUR SECOND-GRADE VALENTINE'S DAY PARTY AND I RAN HOME TO GET YOU A NEW PAIR, OKAY??"

The silence from the other side of the door stretched out for an eternity. I knew I'd been sworn to secrecy on that one—but come on. Desperate times call for desperate measures. When the answer came back, the tone was icy.

"Come on in."

I quietly unlocked the door and opened it. Everyone had been gathered around the door, but quickly backed up when they saw me—just in case. For a moment they just stared.

Mrs. Littlepig was the first to step forward. She reached out and touched the side of my wolf muzzle.

I laughed. Mrs. Littlepig was the only person other than my mom who still called me that. "Hi, Mrs. Littlepig. It's me."

Kevin tried to come over and thank me, but I could see that part of his brain was still arguing that there was a wolf standing in front of him. Finally, he dashed in and gave me a quick hug—then promptly passed out.

After he came back around, I made a quick check of everyone to make sure they were okay. Miss Flett said she had some bruises from being grabbed at the festival, but assured me she'd gotten some pretty good punches and kicks in on the wolf that nabbed her as well.

I quickly laid out my plan for getting us out of there and assured them that we wouldn't get a better chance than right then. Two minutes later, we were creeping as quietly as we could down the hall to the back stairs.

· 20 ·

A LATE-
NIGHT BITE

We had to stop a couple of times on the stairs because of a few small squeaks from floor-boards and one bigger squeak from Kevin. When we reached the bottom, I checked the route to the back door. The guard there was flipping through a Rapunzel's Secret catalog—and very much awake. Which meant we'd have to make our way through the kitchen to the front and hope for a snoozy guard there.

One by one, we slipped around the corner into the laundry room, unheard. When we'd all regrouped, I led everyone into the dark kitchen. We were feeling our way along the counter when the door of the refrigerator against the other wall opened, casting the room in light.

We all dropped to our hands and knees behind the counter, but someone bumped the floor too hard and it made a thump. I cringed, holding my breath.

"Who's there?" I knew that deep growly voice all too well. My heart kicked up to a speedy gallop.

I saw no choice, so I popped up from behind the counter like I'd tripped. "Oops, ha-ha. Clumsy me!"

Silhouetted in front of the fridge was Big Bad, wearing a big fluffy robe and holding a plate of turkey legs and salami.

Oddly, my first thought was that he must have brought his own robe with him, cause Stan Little-pig's robes would have barely covered one of his arms. Then I heard Goldie in my ear, yelling, "Code Red, everyone! Stand by!"

As he stepped over and flipped on the kitchen lights, I felt one of my friends brush my leg as they huddled up closer to the counter.

"The old sandman wouldn't come . . . Couldn't sleep . . ." I was babbling again—and suddenly my ears were itching like crazy.

Big Bad stood there staring at me with a look of disgust. Finally he rolled his eyes and came to the other side of the kitchen counter. He pulled a stool out with his hind paw and settled down just across from me. He leaned over the plate, grabbed a turkey leg in one hand and the salami in the other, and started going to town on them.

I was frozen, staring at his teeth ripping that meat apart, when I felt my ears droop. I reached up and felt one and realized immediately what was happening. My wolf ears had reverted to troll ears!

Big Bad looked up with a mouth full of food. "Are you jush gonna shtan' there an' . . . What happened to your ears?"

I broke out in a sweat as my scalp started to itch and tingle. "It's a . . . a condition."

DROOPY... EAR SYNDROME?

Big Bad grunted and went back to devouring his plate of meat.

In my earpiece, I heard Chester's announcement. "The ears have drooped, people! The ears have drooped!"

I was trying to figure out what to do—how to get the pigs and Miss Flett out of the room—when tufts of orange hair started springing out of the top of my head.

ZOING!

SPROING!

I should have had more time! Rebb must have done the spell wrong!

I covered my head awkwardly just as Big Bad looked up—looking really irritated this time.

"Seriously. Can you move alo . . . ?" He tipped his head to the side. "What are you doing?"

My tail and my snout started to shiver and itch, and I knew I had to get out of there. But Big Bad struck out as fast as a snake and grabbed my arm. He pulled my paw away from my head and was staring at the hair there when my tail disappeared with a big FLOOMP sound.

Big Bad looked confused and started to move backward, standing up off of his stool, when my muzzle popped back to a troll nose in a small puff of smoke.

Big Bad backed into the counter behind him, knocking over several glasses full of used silverware. Amid the clattering, his stunned face dissolved into a snarl.

With one step, he launched himself over the counter at me, growling. As he grabbed me by the shoulders of my jacket, he looked down and saw Miss Flett and the pigs. His eyes went wide and he let out a roar of pure rage.

Big Bad threw me across the kitchen as easily as if I'd been a box of instant porridge. I crashed across the kitchen table and landed in a tangle of chairs and place settings in the corner, listening to Sierra cutting in and out in my ear.

I looked under the table and saw the wolf coming around the counter at the others, blocking their way to the front of the house. I hoisted myself up on one arm and yelled as loud as I could. "GOOOO!!" Kevin and the others scrambled to their feet and took off for the back stairs.

Big Bad rounded the counter and took a swipe at Mr. Littlepig, missing him by millimeters. I heard bedroom doors opening and big paws thudding down the front stairs as the wolves came running. I threw a chair off of me—troll blood and anger starting to fire through my system—and scrambled over the table after them.

I made it halfway through the laundry room before Big Bad caught me. He reached forward and grabbed my hair in one giant fist. I'm not gonna lie to you—it hurt. A lot.

The wolf turned the corner to the stairs at full speed, dragging me behind him like a rag doll—I smashed into the banister and felt my nose hit every spindle on the way up.

We rounded the corner into the upstairs hallway just as the door to Kevin's room slammed shut. Two wolves appeared at the other end of the hall. Big Bad waited impatiently as one unlocked the door before he slammed it open. He yanked the leather jacket off of me and threw me into the room, then loomed in the doorway—his chest rising and falling like he was going to explode. I was on my back and looking at an upside-down version of a nightmare.

Big Bad let out a howl of disgust and anger that shook the whole house. Then he turned around and backhanded one of the wolves behind him—making the smaller wolf yelp and scramble away.

"How did this happen?? I want three of you morons on this door! Do you understand?" Then Big Bad slammed the door shut and we listened to his footsteps as he stormed off down the hall, knocking picture frames off the wall.

No one said a word for a few moments as we caught our breath (and Kevin tried to stop hyperventilating). I listened for the sound of the door being locked again before I spoke.

OKAY. THAT COULD HAVE GONE BETTER.

·21·

No Way Out

...DON'T WANNA BE WOLF BACON...

...FILTHY CLAWS...

It was Kevin's vacant muttering in the corner that snapped me back into action. He was mumbling something about how wolf fangs were covered in dangerous bacteria, and I was worried he'd snapped.

Miss Flett was doing her best to calm Kevin's sister, Ima. I saw Ima was clutching something in her fist and got a lump in my throat when I realized it was a little troll doll I'd given her over the summer.

Kevin's mom was rubbing his back. I was awkwardly getting to my feet when Kevin's dad, Stan, leaned out and grabbed me by the arm.

THANK YOU FOR TRYING, ZARF. YOU'RE A BRAVE TROLL.

Between the disappointment at being back in this room, the pain in my scalp and nose, and the sincerity in his voice, something gave way. I felt my eyes go all blurry with tears and turned away toward the window. I needed to busy myself or I was going to start blubbering like a baby.

I whispered into my wrist.

OKAY. WE, UM... DID YOU GUYS HEAR ALL THAT?

I waited, but no one answered. I tried again and heard nothing. I stuck my finger into my ear to check for the earpiece and realized it was empty. Dropping back to the floor, I started feeling all over for it.

"My earpiece! Help me look!" Mr. Littlepig got down and helped . . . but it wasn't there. It must have fallen out when I was bouncing nose-first up the stairs.

I wouldn't have thought it possible, but my mood plummeted even further. It would have been a perfect moment for a big clap of thunder if this were a movie.

We were on our own.

I crawled up onto the top bunk and flopped down with my face in a pillow to think. And okay, maybe to pout a little. I shivered, and missed that awesome leather jacket. I went to pull a sheet over me when I realized there wasn't one on the bed. I was lying on a bare pillow and mattress. I hung my head over the side of the bed.

HEY, KEV. WHERE'S THE SHEETS?

Kevin rubbed his snout and slowly looked up at me, dazed. "They took them when they took all our cell phones and stuff. Took all the clothes in the closet, too. Basically, anything we could have tied together to climb down the side of the house."

I looked over at the small, dark window. Dang. These wolves weren't as dumb as they looked. I knew it was two stories down to the concrete patio. And not normal stories. Mansion stories, with super-high vaulted ceilings—which made it more like three or four normal stories. I guess these are the things you don't consider when planning your mansion.

I lay there thinking about it as the minutes ticked by. Come on, brain. (Asking a troll brain to come up with a brilliant plan is about like asking a fish to take up jogging.)

Suddenly I had it. I jumped down off the bed. "Okay. Okay. Here's what we do. We shove the mattresses out the window and jump out onto them!"

Kevin just shook his head and looked down at his feet. It was Miss Flett who spoke up.

"Even if the mattresses would fit through the window, which I doubt, there are motion sensors all over the yard. The yard lights would come on as soon as we dropped them. That yard would be Wolf City in three seconds."

Kevin started wailing like a busted foghorn. "Ohhhh . . . We're trapped like Swamp Rats in a cheese bog!"

Mrs. Littlepig gently shushed her kids. "I'm afraid Kevin has a point this time, Zarf."

I felt my shoulders fall as I realized they were right.

There was really and truly no way out of this room.

Until someone knocked on the window.

I'll admit that I jumped a little.

I ran to the window and was startled to find Sierra smiling back at me, upside down.

She motioned for me to open the window. I did, as quietly as I could, and helped her as she swung around and dropped onto the ledge.

Kevin jumped up from the bed, eyes wide.

She put her hand on Kevin's shoulder and spoke as quietly as she could. "Yeah, ding-dong. I'm Supergirl. Hadn't I told you?" She gave him a warm smile to calm him down a bit. "But seriously, we need to scoot, like, pronto."

"How did you . . . ? What? How the . . . ?" I was so flabbergasted, I couldn't put a sentence together.

She smiled as she pulled her backpack off of her shoulder. (I mean seriously, was she planning on doing some homework?)

"Goldie used a crossbow to make the shot of the century while the wolves were distracted. It was seriously amazeballs. She shot a lasso over one of the vent pipes on the roof. As the lightest one of our group, I got to come across. Take a look."

I looked out the window. The rope led away from the roof just above our window to the Ferris wheel, maybe twenty-five yards away. I saw movement in the dark and barely made out the forms of Chester and Goldie waving from the top of the wheel—silhouetted against the dark sky.

When I turned back, Sierra was all business. She pulled a pile of thick gloves out of her pack and tossed them to the others in the room. "These may be a little big, but they'll help you keep a grip on the rope—'cause, y'know . . . falling would be bad."

I watched Kevin's face as he processed this.

"Wait a second."

WE'RE GOING OUT ON THAT ROPE OF DEATH?!?

Thankfully, it was a whisper-yell, but we all shushed him just the same. Sierra took him calmly by the shoulders. "Cool your jets, Kevin. It's the only way over the motion sensors. Any other way out, the wolves will know."

Kevin—mouth hanging open, eyes wide—looked around the room at each of us like we'd lost our minds.

WHAT IF WE FALL??

"What if the wolves on guard just happen to . . . oh, I don't know . . . look up??"

Sierra walked over and moved a side table under the window as a stepping stool.

"Well . . . let's just really, really hope they don't."

· 22 ·

PIGS ON THE LINE

OH, MY.

Mrs. Littlepig was the first out the window after everyone had grabbed some quick hugs. She was shaking, but her face was amazingly composed as she gripped the rope with her gloved front hooves. We all held our breath as she began to scoot herself, hoof over hoof, out over the drop. Kevin gripped the windowsill with white knuckles as he watched.

Mr. Littlepig and Ima went next, with Ima harnessed to Stan's chest using my belt. Ima asked Kevin to put her troll doll in his pocket so she wouldn't lose it. He gave her a kiss on the cheek and took the doll. Then Miss Flett insisted Kevin go next.

He was shaking like a leaf. Sierra and I insisted Miss Flett go while I calmed him down. There was some back and forth—Miss Flett insisting that as the teacher she needed to be the last out—but Sierra and I got really stubborn really fast. We dug our heels in and eventually got our protesting teacher out on the rope.

I grabbed Kevin by the shoulders. "Kev. Do I need to remind you who the pig is?"

He shivered and looked away. "Yeah, yeah. I'm the pig. That's not gonna cut it this time, Zarf."

I squatted down in front of him. "All right, Kevin. If you can't do this for you, do it for your family. They need you. Or for me! I need you to get out of here alive! What if I didn't have you to sweat the small stuff for me?"

CAN YOU IMAGINE?

Kevin sniffed and stared back at me.

"If you're not around, who's gonna stop me from eating sun-warmed mayonnaise? Who's gonna make sure I have Purell at lunch so I don't catch the plague and die? Who's gonna remind me when we have a test in Fable-ometry?"

Kevin chuckled. "It's true."

YOU ARE SORT OF HOPELESS WITHOUT ME.

"You're darn right I am!" I was really going for it. "And I'm just about to enter my teens! Imagine the sort of awful stuff I could get into without you around to keep me in check!"

Kev suddenly looked serious. "You're right. I can't leave you alone with Chester's nutball way of life!" He stood up and cracked his hoof knuckles.

He hopped up to the windowsill, grabbed on to that rope, and backed himself out of the room before we could even help him. He hooked his little legs and was off.

I leaned out the window and whispered after him.

"Yeah, yeah." He didn't look back, but I could tell he was grinning in spite of his fear. "Blow it out your . . ."

And that's when I saw Ima's troll doll slip from his pocket.

I'm not sure why time slows down in moments like this, but watching that doll fall is proof to me that it does. Sierra was beside me as it fell, and she gasped. The motion detectors!

Maybe the hair on that little doll acted as a parachute, because I swear it took five heart-stopping seconds to fall to the patio. It landed and bounced to a stop, and I thought we were okay.

For maybe a split second.

When the lights came on, they came on all at once, and it was blinding. There were floodlights at the base of the house, in the trees, on poles, and under the gutters. The yard lit up like the fifty yard line of the Dragon Bowl.

KAZILLION-
WATT BULB

Immediately, I heard yelps and barks from startled wolves throughout the house. I shout-whispered at the group on the rope, "GO! GO! GO!" and turned to Sierra. "You have to go now!"

But she just looked back at me calmly, with a weird grin. "No way, Zarf. You're going."

I NEED TO FINISH WHAT MY MOM STARTED.

I froze.

Just then I heard huge footsteps pounding down the hallway and the Big Bad Wolf shouting at the top of his lungs. "THE PIGS ARE ESCAPING! GO AFTER THEM! EVERY LAST ONE OF YOU!"

There was a thunderous kick to the door, but the lock held. Sierra pushed me toward the window. "Go, Zarf."

My knees were trembling as the wolf kicked the door again, but I stood my ground. "I'm staying."

Sierra sighed—but bent over and pulled open her backpack. She took out two white balls wrapped in plastic and handed me one. One whiff told me what they were. Then she tugged out a balled-up piece of red fabric.

She looked up at me and rolled her eyes. "Stop looking at me like I've gone goofy, Z. When I was little, my mom trained me to deal with—"

Another kick shattered the top hinge of the door as I heard wolf barks and howls from the yard. From outside, I also heard the shouts of the SQUAT team and the *thwang* sounds of their bows and arrows. I imagined there was a full-scale SQUATist/wolf battle going on in the manor's lawn.

Sierra unrolled the fabric, which turned out to be an old hooded cape—and I knew immediately whose it had been originally. Lastly, she pulled out a large dagger and squared off toward the door.

COME ON IN, LITTLE DOGGIE.

One more kick splintered the door down the middle, and Big Bad burst into the room. His crazed eye did a sweep of the room and froze when it fell on Sierra.

He chuckled—a low, evil sound. There was suddenly pure hate in his eyes, like I've never seen. "Well, hello little lady."

REMATCH

Behind my back, I unwrapped the white ball, and the scent of blue cheese hit me almost immediately.

Sierra took a step toward the wolf. "My, what a mangled-looking ear you have."

Big Bad clearly didn't like this. He took a step forward. "The better to . . . um . . ." I said he was scary, but I never said he was quick with a come-back. "The better to only kind of hear . . . no . . ."

Then he caught a whiff of the cheese ball behind my back.

"OH!" He pulled the lapel of his leather jacket up over his nose. "That is just foul. What . . . ? Is that blue cheese?"

I stepped up as I pulled it out from behind my back. "You'd better believe it."

Big Bad straightened up and tried to act like it didn't bother him, but I saw his throat hitch a couple times like he was gonna hurl.

"But I'm not some—*urk!*—common wolf who can be stopped with a wad of—*retch!*—cheese."

His eyes never left the cheese in my hand, so I had a pretty good idea it was freaking him out.

Sierra was gathering confidence. "Looks like my mom tuned you up pretty good. Why don't you come over and let me even out those ears for you?"

GIVE YOU A LITTLE TRIM.

Tough talk like that may shake the bad guy's confidence in movies—but in this case it just made things worse. Faster than I could have imagined, the wolf lunged for Sierra. One huge paw lashed out and smacked the dagger out of Sierra's hand—and I watched with horror as it flew right out the open window.

FWIP

Sierra went sprawling into the wall, and I dove at the wolf with my ball of cheese. I smashed it into the side of his face, and noted with pride that a good portion went into his ear.

Big Bad recoiled and roared.

DID YOU JUST....? IN MY EAR?? THAT IS SO — URK — WHO DOES THAT??

He was shaking his head and smacking his palm on it like a swimmer with water in his ear. Sierra took the opportunity to unwrap her ball of cheese, lunge forward, and ram it straight up Big Bad's nose.

The huge wolf reacted with the strangest mix of fury and disgust I've ever seen. He bared his fangs, roared, and swatted Sierra across the side of her head—but then fell back snorting and huffing like Chester's dog does when he eats peanut butter.

YOU STUPID LITTLE... SCHNOOOORT! FFFPHTT!!!

I turned and grabbed a lamp off of Kevin's bedside table. It was shaped like his favorite circus clown, Stucco, but I thought he'd forgive me. I hauled off and smashed that lamp as hard as I could over the distracted wolf's head. Big Bad fell back onto one elbow, dazed—and I saw our chance.

I yelled at Sierra to get going out the window. I could see part of her wanted to stay and fight—but a couple of good swats from Big Bad had shaken her pretty bad. She just nodded and scrambled out the window.

The wolf was getting to his back paws as I climbed up to go out the window right behind her. I felt him grab for me at the last second and had to dive out for the rope.

I grabbed on as tight as I could, but the cheese all over my paws made the rope slippery. I almost dropped off as I fought to kick my legs up to grab on.

When I finally had a good grip, I fell in right behind Sierra, going paw after paw as fast as I could. In the yard, the last of the wolves were being chased, yelping, off into the woods by the SQUAT team. Sierra and I were maybe ten feet out when I dared to look back.

Big Bad came crashing through the window, splintering the frame as he squeezed his considerable shoulders through the opening. One of the shutters came loose, and I watched with horror as it fell to the patio below and shattered into four or five pieces.

Sierra and I were picking up the pace when the wolf leaped from the roof and grabbed the rope in one quick, graceful move. We both hooked ourselves around the rope and held on for dear life as it bucked and jumped around like a Flopping Goop-Walrus. (I've only seen a Flopping GoopWalrus on TV, but they're supposed to be super-hard to ride.)

While I waited for the rope to settle down, I was able to look forward and see that Kevin and the others had made it to the Ferris wheel. Goldie and Chester were still in the top seat, urging us on, but the others were scrambling down the emergency ladder on one of the supports.

I felt the rope bouncing and looked back. Big Bad was coming at us at an alarming rate—like scrambling along under ropes was a walk in the park for him.

I saw and heard an arrow fly past the wolf. Then another. Goldie was trying to take him out.

And then he was close enough to reach out for me. I saw his big paw coming and kicked out as hard as I could, knocking it away. I ended up letting my feet drop from the rope so I could use both legs to kick. Then he let go with his front paws and grabbed me around the legs.

This is probably tough to picture in your head, so here's a sketch I did to show you what kind of a situation we ended up in.

WELL... CRUD.

GRR!

Seeing the predicament I was in, Sierra yelled for me to hold on—and started working to climb up onto the rope.

"Hang on, Zarf. Just haaang on, buddy."

Then, in an amazing move that I only half saw, she got to her feet, crouched low with her arms out wide like a tightrope walker. She took one small step, bringing her to where I was holding on. She went to step past my paws and it unbalanced her. Realizing she was going to fall, she dove over me and landed on the rope next to the wolf's legs.

"Hang on, Zarf—like your life depends on it. 'Cause . . . y'know . . . it probably kinda does."

Thanks to the troll blood now going through my

system, I was able to pull myself up and get my arms around the rope.

"Mr. Wolf and I are about to have some fun."

Sierra grabbed one of his back paws.

· 24 ·

THE HARDER
THEY FALL

Apparently, Sierra's mom, Red, had trained her well. She skipped right past tickling and went straight to pulling out the tufts of fur between Big Bad's paw pads. Big Bad started yelping and cursing at her as he kicked his legs, trying to knock her loose.

But Sierra wasn't going anywhere. "This is for my grandmother.

"And this is for my mother, and the life on the run you forced her to live. And this is for me and the normal childhood I never had and for making my mom bring me to live with my HORRIBLE AUNT!"

Okay . . . Clearly Sierra was working through some stuff.

I heard Big Bad yelp and saw his feet slip, so I had a brief warning before my arms almost got pulled out of their sockets—and I was supporting the wolf's weight as well as my own.

His big arms started to pull on my wolf-jeans, and I thought, "If I'm going to die, please let me at least have pants on." I could almost hear Sten Vinders now.

As the full weight of the wolf settled in, I heard the joints in my shoulders groan and let out a couple of gross pops. I was either going to have to let go or my arms were going to get pulled off. I looked down and saw we were above the tents of the darkened festival. In fact, the Dunk-a-Wolf booth was pretty close down there. If I started swinging, I might be able to aim for it.

That's when I felt the first thud. Something slammed into the wolf, and I felt the vibration through my body.

I looked down in time to see a full quart-sized can of Smutton smack into the side of Big Bad's head.

I looked to where the cans were coming from. And there, thirty or forty feet below me, was Kevin—the pitching wonder. He was standing next to an open freezer, throwing cans as fast as he could.

"HAVE SOME ARTIFICIAL MEAT, YOU BIG SACK OF FLEAS!!"

An extra-large can exploded as it made impact with the wolf's shoulder, and I felt his grip loosen for a second.

"STOP IT PIG, OR YOU'RE NEXT!" Big Bad's claws were out and he was digging into me trying to get a better grip. Suddenly I was less worried about getting pantsed than getting skinned.

I looked back in time to see Kevin pull out the largest can yet. He went into his dunk booth Zen trance as Big Bad hurled his insults.

"You're BACON! Do you HEAR ME? I will eat you and your whole stupid family if you don't stop throwing that disgusting fake meat at once!!"

In a blur, Kevin wound up and let rip with that can. I knew before impact that it was a bull's-eye. It caught Big Bad square between the eyes, and I swear I saw his eye turn into a pinwheel something I thought only happened in cartoons.

As he fell, I had a quick thought about this being the ultimate wolf dunk booth. Big Bad somersaulted through the air toward the tank, which seemed like a really appropriate place for him to wind up.

But then I realized the trajectory wasn't quite right. With a sound like a gunshot, Big Bad's shoulder crashed into the steel lip of the dunk tank and he crumpled like a rag doll. So did the tank.

There was a huge explosion of glass and water as the wolf landed upside down on the ground and 300 gallons of water rushed over his limp form. He twitched and whimpered a couple of times and then went still.

Score one for the pig!

I was too exhausted and in too much pain to cheer as Sierra helped me get my legs up and wrapped around the rope. I could hear Chester going nuts—whooping and yelling and yahooing—but all I could focus on was getting off of that rope.

Slowly, we made our way to the big wheel. Chester crawled out and helped us the last twenty feet or so. As he and Goldie pulled me into the top car, I collapsed into the seat with Sierra right behind me. My arms were somehow both numb and throbbing. I felt Goldie, sitting with Chester on the railing behind our little car, ruffle my hair and heard her call out.

"Bring us down, Mr. Littlepig, if you'd be so kind!"

There was some yelling and scurrying around on the ground before the ride came to life. It lurched, and the out-of-tune calliope music started up as we slowly began to descend.

Sierra, leaning against me, reached up and flicked my nose.

I realized, somewhere in the back of my over-worked brain, that I was finally getting that Ferris wheel ride with Sierra—but I was too busy trying not to barf to enjoy it.

Okay . . . That's not true.

I enjoyed it a little.

· 25 ·

SAME AS
IT EVER WAS

We hobbled our way over to where Miss Flett and the Littlepigs had gathered around the fallen wolf. Mr. Littlepig had grabbed a support rope from one of the tents and was using it to tie the groaning wolf's big paws behind his back. I noticed he was tying them extra-tight—really putting his back into it.

I heard my mom's voice and turned as she, my

dad, and Gramps ran out of the woods—my mom leaving a trail of used Kleenex behind her. She was crying so hard, I could barely understand her. "Oh, Zarf. We came as soon as we heard what was going on." Then she swept me up in a huge hug.

I'M SO GLAD YOU'RE OKAY!

It was a sweet moment, until she let go and started swatting me with her purse. "Why do you do this to me? I swear you'll give me a heart attack before you're out of middle school." I had a paw up, shielding her light blows, when I saw my dad and Gramps behind her—all but bursting with pride. My dad gave me a smile and wrapped a SQUAT blanket around my shoulders as Gramps pulled my mom away.

"I think th' boy's been through enough withou' you beatin' him to death with yer handbag."

Kevin walked over and—without saying a word—got Sierra and me in a hug. Feeling a little awkward, I gave him as much of a hug back as my ruined arms would allow.

"That's a heck of an arm you've got there, buddy." Kevin stepped back and hiked up his pants.

It was such an un-Kevin thing to say, I had to laugh—though the laughing hurt and I realized I might have a busted rib or two.

Mr. Littlepig was tying up Big Bad's feet when I heard a winded voice coming down the hill behind me. You know—THAT voice. The sniveling one.

"I . . . I command you apprehend this wolf-beast at once! On my orders! As the commanding officer of this operation!"

I cringed and turned around. Prince Roquefort was running up—and I couldn't believe my eyes.

Everyone stood staring at him. He was still in the process of turning back from a teapot and the effect was pretty unsettling.

"WHAT?!" He looked furious and maybe just a touch panicked. "What are you all gaping at?"

He zeroed in on me. I'll admit I was having trouble stifling a laugh.

"If I had arms I would throttle the living daylights out of you!"

And that did it. We all broke up. I've never been thankful for the prince before or since, but that cut through the tension and we all dissolved into laughter—which of course enraged the teapot-prince even further. He started stomping around and huffing and puffing.

When two members of the SQUAT team came back from chasing the other wolves, they found a bound villain, a steaming-mad half-pot prince, and a yard full of us sitting on the ground, wiping away tears of laughter.

I'd love to tell you that we all returned to school to a hero's welcome, but I think we've come far enough that you know that's not the way we roll here in Cotswin.

No, school the next day was pretty much business as usual—except for the buzz in the air that the Big Bad Wolf was alive and well. That had everyone pretty good and freaked out.

As I was making my way to my locker, Sten Vinders came up behind me and slipped a live, flopping Lumpy Snapper down the back of my shorts.

If there was some kind of symbolism to the fish in the pants, I missed it—but Sten has never been known for his keen wit. In a weird way, I took it as him saying thanks in the only way he knew how . . .

On my way into Miss Flett's class, I passed Sierra.

She stopped and we looked at each other for an extra-long moment, smiling knowingly.

Sierra tucked a stray wisp of hair behind her ear. "Yeah. We're hoping word of Big Bad being alive and his capture get to my mom—wherever she is. But she can't come back, even if she's still . . . you know . . . alive. There's still a lot of wolves out there, and they hold grudges worse than a sixth-grade Cheer-Maiden."

"Yeah, great." I swallowed hard, realizing we were both probably on a wolf hit list somewhere.

"So you're stuck with your aunt for now?"

She shrugged. "For the meantime. But now that the Big Grand Secret's out, she seems like she's being a little nicer. She's fine . . . She's just not my mom."

We stood there thinking about that for a long moment.

Then she hauled off and gave me a friendly punch in the arm and went on in to her seat.

I laughed and went on in too, and sat there rubbing my arm where she'd hit me until I caught myself and stopped.

I glanced over at the prince, but he was sitting low in his chair, staring straight ahead.

Miss Flett blew into the room just before the bell rang. She set her purse and bags down on her desk and turned to the class with a warm smile.

"You honestly have no idea how happy I am to be back."

Then she addressed Chester, Kevin, Sierra, and me. "I spoke to John this morning. He's back, and he said someday soon, he'll figure out how to thank you all properly."

Just then the PA system gave off a squeal of feedback, and we could hear Principal Haggard clearing his throat.

I won't bore you with the whole long thing. He thanked those of us who participated in taking down Big Bad as well as a number of other wolves. He gave us an update that the SQUATists had captured most of the wolf gang, and chased the others back past Snuff's Pillow—leaving the ones that got away with a few arrows in their backsides as souvenirs.

The captured wolves had been thrown into the kingdom's dungeon system for the time being. As for Big Bad himself, he was in a maximum-security dungeon under constant surveillance. Additional measures had been taken to ensure he would never get free.

Then he blathered on for a while about what a great school and student body we had and blah blah blah.

When the announcement was over, Miss Flett just sat on the desk and smiled at us all for a bit.

Finally, she clapped her hands on her thighs and stood up. "Okay! Let's get things back to normal! Pull out your books and flip to chapter fifteen."

I opened the top of my desk to get my book out, and heard a strangled little gasp from my right. I looked over and the prince was staring down into his desk. Anger flashed across his features as he reached in and pulled out a single teabag.

Then he reached in and started pushing teabag after teabag out onto the floor. Leaning just a bit, I could see that someone had literally filled his desk with the things. He pulled out his book and maybe thirty bags fell out.

Behind me, I heard Chester.

The room was quiet for just a second as I spun in my chair to face Chester. He gave me a wink so fast, I almost missed it.

My jaw was hanging open in total shock as the entire class let go and started laughing—and Prince Roquefort struggled down from his seat and stormed out of the room.

I couldn't believe it, but I had to admit it. It was happening.

Chester was getting funnier.

THE END

ABOUT
THE AUTHOR

Rob Harrell created and drew the internationally syndicated comic strip *Big Top*, as well as the acclaimed graphic novel *Monster on the Hill*. He also writes and draws the long-running daily comic strip *Adam@Home*. He survived middle school and now lives with his wife in Austin, Texas. Visit his website at www.lifeofzarf.com.